Trouble in the Town Hall

Also by Jeanne M. Dams

The Body in the Transept

TROUBLE IN THE TOWN HALL

A Dorothy Martin Mystery

JEANNE M. DAMS

WALKER AND COMPANY
NEW YORK

Many people helped with the research for this book, but I owe special thanks to Sir Robert Bunyard, retired Chief Constable of the county of Essex, for his invaluable expertise about the intricacies of English police procedure. If I've made mistakes, it is despite his excellent advice.

First published in the United States of America in 1996 by Walker Publishing Company, Inc.

Published simultaneously in Canada by Thomas Allen & Son Canada, Limited, Markham, Ontario

Library of Congress Cataloging-in-Publication Data
Dams, Jeanne M.
Trouble in the town hall: a Dorothy Martin mystery/Jeanne M. Dams.
p. cm.
ISBN 0-8027-3285-2 (hardcover)
I. Title.
PS3554.A498T76 1996
813′ 54—dc20 96-26485
CIP

Printed in the United States of America
2 4 6 8 10 9 7 5 3 1

To my mentor and biggest fan,
my wardrobe adviser and best friend,
my surrogate mother—
to the woman who is all those things,
my sister, Betty

Prologue

THE CLOUDLESS HEAVENS had just begun to pale over the ancient cathedral town of Sherebury. As the last few stars flickered out in the brightening sky of that midsummer dawn, England turned its worshiping face to its oldest god, the sun—which divinity, with a beaming benevolence rare in those latitudes, poured out his blessings upon the city. The warm tide of light, paying tribute first to the newer creed, flowed over the topmost cross of the cathedral, washing its cool stone with golden glory, splashing down the spire. Treetops and chimney stacks were warmed and brightened, as were the roofs of the university on the hill and the clock tower of the Town Hall. The clock face showed 4:57.

Minute by minute, as the sun rose higher, its golden rays reached deeper, bathing the humbler roofs, the walls, the windows. In east-facing bedrooms, springs creaked and snores were interrupted as sleepers shifted to keep the brilliance out of their eyes.

The light at last reached the humble, dusty window of a broom closet, shining straight into the open eyes of the man on the floor who lay unblinking, unmoving.

The sunlight, indifferent, continued its stately progress.

1

THE JUNE DAY had started off normally enough with the cats' demands to be fed and let out. They'd been up very early—the birds' response to a brilliant midsummer sunrise had wakened all their hunting instincts—but there was, unfortunately, nothing unusual about that. By six I was functional myself and trying to do something about my flower beds, to the astonishment of my next-door neighbor. She restrained herself, however.

"Quite a job of work you've got there, Dorothy," she said mildly, leaning on the back gate and surveying the dejected-looking flower bed over the top of her glasses with a Churchillian frown.

"Jane Langland, don't you start making caustic remarks." I sat up, with sharp cracks from both knees, and looked over my scraggly flowers and flourishing weeds. "I know I've never been much of a gardener, and maybe I'm a little old to start now. But I've wanted an English garden all my life. Your climate in this country gives people pneumonia, but it does wonders for roses."

"Not doing much for yours," retorted Jane with brutal candor. "Why not find a gardener?"

"Even if I could afford it, the midwestern work ethic would

protest. Frank and I always did things ourselves." And together. I brushed a sudden treacherous tear from my cheek, careless of the mud on my gloves, and Esmeralda woke from her nap in a patch of catnip and came over to rub her comforting, furry gray bulk against my legs.

"Frank loved gardens, too," Jane pointed out briskly. "He told me so, when you two were first thinking of moving here from the States. Said the flowers were the best thing about England. Expect he's up there shaking his head over the hash you're making of this."

"Probably." I managed a grin in appreciation of her unsentimental sympathy. "Anyway, I don't want to commit myself to a gardener while everything is so unsettled. I thought this morning, when those miserable beasts wanted out at the crack of dawn, that I should put in a cat door. But I can't do even a simple thing like that until I own the house, and I'm *not* going to buy it unless I can fix it up, and it looks to me as if this planning thing is going to go on forever." I waved away a heavy, furry bumblebee and bent to my work again, viciously attacking a clump of large leaves while Samantha, my Siamese, chased the bee.

"Planning permission takes weeks," Jane pointed out, "especially for a listed building. I'd engage that gardener, meanwhile. Planning committee's more apt to believe you intend to preserve the character of the house if the garden is lovely and traditional. Which it won't be under your tender care." She chuckled richly in a deep baritone. "That 'weed' you just murdered was a delphinium, you know."

BUT I TOILED stubbornly for the rest of that gorgeous, increasingly hot morning, until the phone call from Alan rescued me. I was delighted to accept a last-minute lunch date with Sherebury's chief constable, who had been so busy with constabulary duties that I'd hardly seen him for the past couple of weeks. So I dolled myself up in a smart new black-and-white dress and my best black straw hat, and sallied forth to do a little shopping before lunch at the new Indian restaurant we'd been wanting to try.

Or at least I tried to sally. A morning spent on my knees hadn't improved either them or my back, and black patent heels are impractical walking shoes for a woman of any age, let alone one who's—well, old enough to know better. So if sallying implies a certain briskness of pace, mine was more of a meander.

It suited the day, anyway. Sherebury High Street was, I thought critically, looking somewhat better than in recent months. The weather had brought out shoppers in droves, and the baskets full of petunias and geraniums hanging from the lampposts looked festive. The cathedral spire, just visible over the shops across the street, positively sparkled against the perfect blue sky.

There was still a certain gap-toothed look to the street, though. Every month or so another shop closed "for renovations" and never reopened. The depressed economy of my adopted town was showing, and I worried about it.

The worst blight of all was the poor old Town Hall, decaying from dry rot and the deathwatch beetle, and most of all from lack of money for repairs. Nothing could spoil its generous Elizabethan proportions, or its exquisite materials and workmanship, but with official city business having moved to a hideous new Civic Centre, the Town Hall exuded the bereft air of the abandoned. The great tubs of flowers that used to flank its studded oak doors had been taken away, the papers fluttering from the notice boards were torn and faded. Streaked, uncurtained windows looked in on a once busy, now deserted interior.

But it wasn't deserted. I stopped just as I was about to pass the building, and stared. I could have sworn I'd seen movement behind one of the windows—there it was again! I moved closer and peered into dimness; I thought I caught a glimpse of something, but then it was gone.

I tried the door—locked, just as it should be. Certainly it was no business of mine, but a confirmed snoop is never put off by a little thing like that. I knocked.

The shadow came closer. "Round to the side door! I 'aven't got me key to the front!"

The voice, female and strongly Cockney, reassured me utterly. Obviously she belonged there (and I did not), but I was committed now. Feeling silly, I went obediently to the side door, a dreary little portal I had never noticed before, opening onto the narrow passageway between the Town Hall and the modern building next door.

A large gray-haired woman stood in the doorway, dustcloth in hand. Appraising my going-out-to-lunch dress and hat, she spoke doubtfully. "Was you wantin' somethin', madam? On account of, there's nobody 'ere no more, you know."

"I know," I agreed apologetically. "I'm sorry to bother you, but when I saw someone in here I wondered—I mean, I didn't know the building was still being kept clean, Mrs.—?"

"Ada Finch. And as for keepin' it clean, that's in a manner of speakin', that is. Come in, then, luv." Seizing the opportunity for conversation, she led me round to the staircase in the front hall, settled herself with a comfortable grunt on the third step, and took up where she'd left off. "In the old days I'd 'ave bin 'ere at 'alf past five, to get everything spic *and* span for them as worked 'ere. Now, o' course, it's just keepin' the woodwork nice for them as is goin' to move in, so I only 'as a day now and again, and 'oo knows 'ow long that'll keep on." She fetched a gusty sigh from beneath the layers of sweaters that covered her ample bosom. "Breaks me 'eart, it does, to see the place like this after all the years I looked after it lovely."

"The woodwork is still beautiful, though. The carving on that staircase is in perfect condition."

"Never a crack in it," said Mrs. Finch triumphantly, giving the elaborate spiked newel post an affectionate rub with her rag, "for all it is 'undreds of years old. Lovely piece of work, that staircase is. Carved all the way to the top, and every landin' different. Makes a lot of work, but I keeps it nice. You should 'ave seen the job I 'ad, too, cleanin' it proper when I first come to work 'ere. More years ago than I care to remember, that was, and me just a young girl workin' under that sour old Mr. Jobbins." She sniffed. "More concerned about gettin' 'is tea regular than keeping the place up to snuff, 'ee was. Young I might've bin, but I knew better than to let the dust pile up in all them crevices. I bin trained right. Went at it with a nail file, I did, and sometimes a toothpick, month after month, until I 'ad it lookin' like new. Polishes up a treat, don't it?"

"It's magnificent," I said sincerely. "It's such a pity—"

"That's wot I says," Mrs. Finch broke in eagerly. "Terrible shame it'll be if that Mr. Pettifer and them pull it all about and turn it into one of them malls. I don't 'old with shoppin' malls. Give me proper shops, where you could 'ave a talk with the butcher, or greengrocer as it might be, friendly-like, and maybe get a nice little piece of liver for the cat, or a wilted lettuce, and do 'im a favor next time out.

"Ah, well, them days is gone forever; you've got to move with the times or get left behind. Speakin' o' time—" Mrs. Finch looked at the man's wristwatch shoved far up on her left arm. "I always 'as me a cuppa just about now. Would you like one, Mrs.—?"

"Martin, Dorothy Martin," I said hastily. "I'm sorry, I should have introduced myself. And thank you, but I'm supposed to be meeting someone; I really have to—"

"You're American, ain't you?" she said as she clumped to a closet behind the stairs. "I've 'eard as 'ow they don't drink tea. Dunno 'ow they get through the day. Time was when I could 'ave a nice cuppa with me mates, the rest o' the cleaners, sit in comfort in a room they give us, put me feet up and 'ave a bit of a gossip. Now I keeps me tea things in the broom cupboard and 'as to make do with sittin' on the stairs by me lonesome, but still, tea's tea."

She opened the door as she spoke and took one step into the tiny room before she caught her breath in a sharp gasp and screamed.

SO IT WAS that, for the second time in six months, I found myself staring into the eyes of a dead man. The first experience, in Sherebury Cathedral on Christmas Eve, was something I didn't care to remember; I'd made a nuisance of myself to all concerned, including my new acquaintance Chief Constable Alan Nesbitt. But perhaps familiarity softens these blows. More likely, I was too taken up with Mrs. Finch's hysterics to have time for any of my own.

After the first frozen moment of shock, poor Mrs. Finch collapsed against the paneled wall of the hallway, gasping and whimpering, and I could get a good look.

On the whole, I wished I hadn't. The man was young, no more than a boy, really. His eyes, horribly, were wide open. I'd seen only that much when we were interrupted.

"Mrs. Finch! What is it?" The voice from somewhere behind us was loud, peremptory, and male, and I yelped. When I turned, heart pounding, and he came closer to our gloomy corner, I recognized him. Oh, marvelous. Archibald Pettifer, city councilman, real estate developer, and self-appointed minder of everyone's business. Just what we needed.

"Mrs. Finch! Mrs.—er—madam! What is the trouble?"

His stentorian bellow finally got through to the cleaning lady, who hiccuped and wobbled away to the stairs, sniffling into her apron. Mr. Pettifer stood for a moment looking down at the body on the closet floor. Then he shook his head like a bull ready to charge and took over.

"Now, then, what is all this?"

His shaking voice and dirty-ivory face belied his pompous attitude, and I nearly giggled. I've met Pettifer on only a couple of occasions, which was enough; he irritates me simply by existing. He must have noticed that I wasn't impressed, because he glared at me and cleared his throat.

"Madam, I am Archibald Pettifer, and I asked a question. What—"

I drew myself up. "I heard you, Mr. Pettifer, and we've met. Dorothy Martin, since you don't seem to remember. I didn't answer because I have no more idea than you. Mrs. Finch opened the door and found that man lying on the floor. He is apparently dead. I don't know who he is or what he's doing here." Two could play the pompous game.

He seized on my last words. "Ah! And what are *you* doing here, may one ask?"

I caught my temper by the tail just as it was about to lash out, claws fully extended. "I saw Mrs. Finch in here, through the window, and came in to make sure there was no problem. And may I point out, sir, that we should be taking care of Mrs. Finch and calling the police instead of questioning each other? I haven't asked why *you* are here, or how you got in."

His look this time ought to have turned me to stone, but he did offer an explanation of sorts. "I—er—heard a scream and came in the side door, which Mrs. Finch had no business to leave unlocked. Furthermore, *I* have legitimate business here. And I was about to suggest that, if Mrs. Finch insists on having hysterics, you take her to some place where she can sit down properly—" he looked about as if expecting a chair to materialize in the hallway "—and then summon the police. Unfortunately, no telephones remain in the building, and someone must stay here with the—to—er—must stand guard."

I seized at the idea of escape. There was a public phone at Debenham's, the big chain department store across the street, which also had a tearoom. I thought I'd have trouble moving Mrs. Finch, but once she took in the word "tea" she forged ahead like a horse nearing its stable.

When I had her settled at the one free table with a pot of tea and some biscuits, I slipped away to the phone. After the emergency 999 call I asked for Alan—an entirely separate office, since his job is purely administrative—and was told he was out to lunch.

Oh, good grief, of course he was—he was waiting for me. That call took a little longer.

"Alan, thank God I found you!" I babbled in relief. "I couldn't remember the name of the restaurant, so I had to talk to your secretary, and she had to call for the number, and—"

"Dorothy." His voice was sharp, official. "Tell me."

"There's been a murder, Alan! At least I think so. It's at the Town Hall, and I was there when—"

"I'll be there."

He hung up and I went back to Mrs. Finch, who had finished one cup of tea and recovered her volubility.

"And wot I'd like to know," she said with a sniff, pouring another cup of repellent black brew and copiously adding milk, "is, 'oo is 'ee, and 'ow did 'ee come to be in *my* cupboard?" Her chins quivered with outraged dignity and her voice rose. " 'Oo-ever 'ee is, 'ee'd no call to come and die 'ere! Look at the trouble 'ee'll cause! And no more than a layabout, to look at 'im."

"You got a close look?" I asked, lowering my voice in the hope that she would do the same, though the lunchtime crowd probably drowned us out.

"Well—not to say *look*. But 'is clothes and all . . . "

I understood. Mrs. Finch had barely glanced at the body before dissolving into hysterics, but she found comfort in the thought that the human being who had once inhabited that body was a stranger and a useless sort of person.

I was not so easily comforted. No matter who the dead man

was or what his life had been, his end was pitiable. Mrs. Finch was certainly right about one thing, though: There was a great deal of trouble ahead for everyone concerned.

"Have you finished your tea? Do you think you're well enough to go talk to the police?"

"Go 'ome and 'ave meself a drop o' gin, is wot I'd like to do," she said wistfully. "Wot a 'ope! They'll be asking their questions till the cows come 'ome. Well, no 'elp for it." She heaved herself to her feet. "Thanks for me tea. Went down a treat; I'm meself again. Sure you won't 'ave any? There's a cup left in the pot."

I shuddered. I probably needed sustenance, and my nice lunch with Alan wasn't going to happen, but I was a little more upset than I liked to admit, and my stomach was in no state to deal with stewed tea. "I'm fine. Shall we go get it over with?"

The police had arrived in the few minutes since I had phoned. A crowd had gathered, but Mrs. Finch sturdily shouldered aside all would-be obstacles. When the constable at the Town Hall door barred our way, she stared him down, hands on formidable hips.

" 'Ere, ducks, I'm the one wot found the body, and they want to talk to me. And this 'ere is Mrs. Martin, and she was with me. So just you get out of the doorway an' let us pass." Fortified by tea, she was beginning to enjoy her importance.

The scene of crime team was already busy inside the building, and just inside the front door Pettifer was arguing with a uniformed policeman. He apparently wanted to talk to the officer in charge, whose whole attention was taken up with directing his men.

Our constable escorted us to the officer in question and murmured something to him.

"Yes?" He looked us over. "I'm Inspector Morrison. I understand one of you ladies discovered the body?"

He was a man of about fifty, inconspicuous-looking save for a very sharp eye and a quick manner that stopped just short of impatience. He gestured us toward the stairs, the only place to sit, and was following when Pettifer accosted him.

"Look here, sir! Am I to be kept waiting about all day? I've told my story twice, what there was to tell, and I've pressing business to attend to. That ass over there said you wanted to talk to me. Well, here I am!" His face was red and his hands were clenched and shaking; I had a fleeting moment of worry about his blood pressure. I may dislike Archibald Pettifer and all his works, but I didn't want him to have a heart attack on the spot.

"Presently, sir. Rest assured we'll not keep you any longer than necessary. If you'd care to wait over there?" The inspector pointed to a spot well out of earshot. Pettifer scowled at all of us and stomped off.

"Now then, ladies?"

We sat down on the hard oak steps, and the inspector turned his attention to me. "You are . . . ?"

"Dorothy Martin. My address is Monkswell Lodge."

His attitude sharpened slightly. "Ah, yes, the American lady. Involved in the cathedral murders, weren't you?"

"Involved is not exactly the word I would choose."

He smothered a smile. "No, perhaps not. Now, what can you tell me about this incident?" The uniformed man by his side began to take notes.

"Very little, I'm afraid. It's Mrs. Finch's story, really." I related how I happened to be in the building and what I'd seen, trying to remember exact times and failing, and feeling very silly about the whole thing, and then it was Mrs. Finch's turn.

She was asked in excruciating detail about every movement she had made since arriving at the Town Hall, and she was pleased to oblige, proudly describing her dusting and polishing of almost every surface that might have been expected to yield evidence. If the inspector winced he tried not to show it; the woman was simply doing her job and couldn't be expected to know what was lurking in the broom closet. It wasn't until she began to add anecdotes about how she had felt in her bones all morning that something was wrong that his fingers began to drum very quietly on the beautifully polished banister.

"Yes, well, thank you, Mrs. Finch. I think that'll be all—or, no, just one more thing. How did you get into the building this morning?"

She bristled at that. "With me key, 'ow do you think?"

"Of course," Morrison said soothingly. "I actually meant, by which door?"

"Oh." Mrs. Finch colored, ducked her head, and gave him a sideways grin. "Sorry, luv. I'm *that* upset—you mustn't take no notice. Come in the side door, same as always. Off Cat Lane?"

The inspector nodded. "And was the door locked?" he went on.

Mrs. Finch looked at him with pity in her blue eyes, her head to one side like an elderly robin's. "Naow. I always wastes me time unlockin' doors as is unlocked already. O' course it was locked!"

"And when you leave—you lock it up again with the key?"

That did it. Mrs. Finch stood up and transfixed the inspector with a look that might have cut through the solid oak paneling. "I'll 'ave you know, Mr. Fancy P'liceman, as Ada Finch 'as never gone off and left a door open in this 'ere ancient monument! Time was I 'ad the keys to every door in this place, leavin' out the big front door, as is barred. And all the keys was different, and big as 'orses. Now the pore old place is left to itself I only 'as the one, and I guards it with me life! 'Ere, see for yourself!"

She fished in her pocket, brought forth a large old-fashioned key all by itself on a ring with a big brass hotel-style tag, and waved it an inch in front of his face. "I put that tag on so's I'd 'ear it fall if I dropped it, and I could find it easy. An' I locks the door every time I leaves, or I'll eat me key, tag an' all, with 'orseradish sauce!"

She folded her arms, her lower lip protruding ominously,

and while the inspector soothed and placated and assured her he didn't doubt her word, I pondered the point about the key. If the place was securely locked up, how had the dead man gotten in? And more to the point, how had the murderer gotten out, leaving a dead bolt locked behind him? Someone inside, presumably the murderer, could have unbarred the ancient front door to let the victim in, but you can't leave by a barred door.

The inspector was winding up with the disgruntled Mrs. Finch. "You've been very helpful, and I'm truly sorry to have kept you here so long. We'll have your statement typed and ask you to come down to the station to sign it, but there is just one more point. Did you, in the course of your work, see or move anything out of the ordinary?"

"Dirt an' rubbish was wot I moved," she snapped. "Look in the dustbin if you like."

I had no doubt he or his men would do just that. I had every doubt they'd find anything of interest.

"I know you must be longing for a bit of rest, Mrs. Finch. We'll let you know when you can resume your work here—soon, of course," he added hastily, seeing her face grow even grimmer. "We must seal the building as a crime scene for now, and I shall have to keep your key for a day or two." He tried a conciliatory smile.

Mrs. Finch was having none of his peacemaking; her honor had been impugned. "And 'oo's goin' to clean up the place, then?" she demanded, hands on hips. "Dustin' for fingerprints, they calls it; I calls it makin' a ruddy great mess! As if I didn't 'ave enough to do, trying to keep this place from goin' to rack and ruin while the muckety-mucks decide what's to be done with it, pore old place, left all any'ow so as they could go and 'ave their fine new offices in that fine new pile o' concrete as'll fall down about their ears in a year or so, I shouldn't wonder, and serve 'em right, too, makin' us common folks traipse out miles from anywhere to fill out their

ruddy forms an' all, and bus fares bein' wot they are, too . . . "
She grumbled her way out the door, heading for her drop of gin
and a glorious gossip with the neighbors.

Inspector Morrison raised an eyebrow and smiled a little at
her retreating back, shaking his head. "A vanishing breed, God
bless her. Salt of the earth, but infuriating at times." He shook
his head again, dismissed Mrs. Finch from his mind, and turned
the full force of those disconcerting gray eyes on me. "Can you
tell me, Mrs. Martin, your impression of Mrs. Finch when she
found the body? Was she truly surprised, or . . . ?"

"If she wasn't flabbergasted and terrified, you can tell the
Queen to hand her a knighthood, or a dameship, or whatever it
is, for being the finest actress in the United Kingdom. I never
saw a more genuine fit of hysteria. Anyway, you only have to
look at her to know she's honest."

"Right." The monosyllable accepted what I'd said, without
necessarily agreeing. "Of course, the one who finds the body is
so often—however. Now, if we can go once more over—"

"Dorothy! There you are! Morning, Morrison, this one fell
to you, eh? Bad luck on such a glorious day!"

Alan, a big man who looks like Alistair Cooke, made an
impressive entrance. I was so glad to see him I looked up with
what must have been a *Perils of Pauline* sort of expression; he
smiled back affably and spoke again to the inspector.

"You haven't met Mrs. Martin, have you, Derek—except
officially, I mean? Pity you had to meet over a corpse, but we
may yet be thankful she was here. You'll find her a good witness,
I believe."

"I had already drawn that conclusion, sir." His eyes soft-
ened. "I was just about to take her through it all again, but
it's probably pointless; she was thorough and concise the
first time. If you'd like . . ." He sketched an "after you" in
Alan's direction.

There was something about his gesture that suggested he

was deferring not only to his superior officer, but to an important friend of the witness. Ah, well, Sherebury is a small town, after all. So he'd known all along I was Alan's—what? Perhaps this was not the moment to try to define the relationship.

"No, indeed, I shan't interfere. But if you've actually finished, I'd like to give the lady some lunch. Dorothy? Do you need to brush yourself down?"

"No, Mrs. Finch keeps the place spotless. I'm just stiff. Is my hat all right?"

"Very nice indeed," he said with the almost hidden smile he addresses to all my hats, and offered me his arm.

I was glad enough to take it; reaction had set in. "Alan, I don't know if I can manage Indian food, after all. My insides are acting a little peculiar."

"I shouldn't wonder, but you do need to eat. How long ago was breakfast?"

"It feels like years."

"Right, then what about something simple and sustaining at Alderney's?"

Alderney's is the tea shop in the Cathedral Close and one of my favorite places in Sherebury. "Perfect. They have wonderful comfort food." He started to move toward the door, but I pulled at his arm.

"Alan, I have to know what they've found out. Did you have a chance to talk to anyone? Who is—he?" I jerked my head toward the broom closet. "Does this have anything to do with the preservationist battle over the Town Hall?"

"No idea. I did have a word with the men before I talked to you, but they don't know much yet. How in the name of all that's holy did you get mixed up in this, by the way?" His voice was quiet, but the concern he wouldn't display in front of Inspector Morrison was apparent.

"Pure accident, and I'm not 'mixed up' in it. I just had the bad luck to be here." I summarized what had happened. "Who is he?" I repeated.

"There was no identification on the body. Young, early twenties probably; you will have gathered that. I don't suppose he was at all familiar to you?"

"I didn't look properly. I could check now, I suppose."

Alan put his hand over mine, still clinging to his arm. "Only if you want to. There's little likelihood you would know him, after all."

"No, it's all right. You're a very reassuring person, you know."

"If you're certain." He took me to the door of the closet and said something to the policemen still working there, who moved aside.

The man lay on his back, arms and legs spread-eagled, filling the floor of the small room. He was dressed in a dirty black T-shirt and a pair of blue jeans, frayed at the knees and not, I thought, on purpose. He looked very young indeed. A scrabble of beard failed to hide a pasty, acne-scarred face. His hair, worn longer than my taste preferred, was of a color hard to determine, so greasy were the locks scattered against the floorboards. His eyes were shut.

"No," I said in a not very steady voice after a long look. I was shaken with pity for a young life ended, and perhaps, from his appearance, unhappy, meaningless even before the final blow of fate. "No, I've never seen him before."

We were on our way out of the building before I spoke again. "Alan, would they—the police, I mean—would they have moved the body?"

"Not at this stage; they haven't finished with photographs. Why?" He was all Chief Constable Nesbitt again.

"Because it's been moved. His arms were down at his sides when I saw him. I didn't see much, but I saw that. And—" I tried to control a shudder "—his eyes were open."

AFTER THAT, of course, Alan stayed to talk to Inspector Morrison and his men for a few minutes, with the result that we hit Alderney's at the height of the lunchtime rush. Alan managed to get us a table. He usually does; I've never been sure whether it's those devastating blue eyes or the fact that a chief constable is an important person, rather like a medieval lord sheriff. It was definitely the eyes, though, that got a pot of tea on the table almost instantly. He poured me a cup and made me add a lot of sugar. He also poured a little brandy in it.

"Alan, you never cease to amaze me! Do you always carry a flask? I've never noticed it."

"Emergency stores only. I bring it when I feel I may be called upon to rescue a swooning lady. Drink that down."

I'd have disputed "swooning lady" if it hadn't been so close to accurate. As it was, I obediently drank my tea, relaxed, and suddenly recovered my senses.

"Alan, the bookshop! My job! What time is it? I have to go—"

"Sit still. I'll ring them up." He untangled his long legs from the maze of table and chairs, spoke to the hostess, and picked up her telephone at the desk.

"What did you say?" I demanded when he got back. "I wouldn't want Mrs. Williamson upset—"

"That you were being detained by the police to assist us with our inquiries."

"Alan, you didn't! She'll have a heart attack!"

"No, I didn't, actually. I said you'd been unavoidably delayed and would be there as soon as possible. I did identify myself."

I sighed. "She'll worry herself into a stew, poor dear. I'd better hurry, so I can explain for myself."

"You'd do better to go home after you've had a spot of lunch. You're still quite white, you know."

"Oh. Well, no, I didn't, but really I'm fine, Alan, or I will be when I've eaten something. I have to get to the bookshop, Mrs. Williamson's counting on me. Anyway, work keeps me from thinking, and the cathedral is such an oasis of calm, I'll feel much better. I'm sure."

I was protesting too much, but Alan let it go and simply said, "Why on earth don't you call the woman by her first name? The English aren't all *that* formal, you know."

"Her first name is Ariadne."

"Oh, dear. Yes, I do see. What do the others call her?"

"Willie. Somehow I can't . . ."

"Quite." He looked at the menu. "How about chicken rolls and rice pudding for both of us? Nursery food."

"Sounds good." And when the sandwiches arrived, crusty rolls with lots of white meat and lettuce, I attacked mine like a starving woman.

"So how," I said when I could speak, "are plans for the royal visit coming along?" I wanted a respite from murder, and I figured Alan was good for several minutes on his chief headache of the moment, the impending visit of Prince Charles to open the new wing of the hospital.

Alan ran a hand down the back of his neck. "As smoothly

as these things ever go, I suppose, actually. It's just that the Palace has got the wind up, rather. And so have I, much as I hate to admit it."

"About what—hecklers about the Diana situation?"

"Not so much that as these damned anarchists." He glanced casually around the room, which was beginning to thin out as those on limited lunch hours hurried off. The table next to ours was empty, but Alan lowered his voice all the same. "I can't be specific, but a recent episode is seen as a direct threat to Prince Charles. They managed to keep it out of the press, but—" He raised his hands in a gesture of exasperation.

"The Prince's people think there'll be a next time?"

"There will be, undoubtedly. The question I must deal with is, Will it be in Sherebury? That's what I want to know from MI5 and the rest of the security lot, what sort of threat I might have to contend with, and so far they've not been able to tell me."

"I can't get over being amazed at the idea of anarchists." I glanced at my plate, surprised to find it empty. Alan's prescription had been admirable. "It all sounds so quaint and dated, straight out of the twenties."

"Doesn't it? Unfortunately the current lot are not at all dated. They organize their little games over the Internet."

"Good grief. Do you really think someone like that might be working in Sherebury?"

Our rice pudding arrived and we both tasted its creamy goodness before Alan replied.

"I don't know—and I should know—but I'm uneasy. I have a feeling something nasty is going on; I just can't put my finger on it." He ran his hand over his neck again and began to tick off points on his fingers. "There's the Town Hall business. Pettifer wants to turn it into his mall; the preservationists are fighting tooth and nail to save it. All right, but it's getting just that much more heated than one would expect. So is the controversy over that university housing scheme of his—did you know Pettifer's received two anonymous letters? No more than vague threats, but it's unusual in a preservation matter; the chattering classes are the ones who care the most, and they don't stoop to such tactics."

"And now—today—"

"Indeed. Can you talk about it now?"

One reason Alan has risen to such a senior police rank is his sensitive understanding of people. It's also one of the reasons I'm so fond of him. I smiled and put down my spoon.

"So long as we avoid the more graphic bits, I want to know what you know."

He sat back and tented his fingers in what I had come to know as his lecturing pose. "Well, I asked, of course, about the body, and got confirmation they hadn't moved it except to look for identification. There was none, as I told you. At that stage they hadn't even taken his fingerprints."

"That means Pettifer, doesn't it? He was alone with—him—" I couldn't make myself call that pitiful creature *it* "—while Mrs. Finch and I went to Debenham's."

"It looks like it. Though why . . . ?" Alan shrugged his massive shoulders. "They'll put him through it, of course, about that and about the question of keys."

"I've thought about that. I don't suppose there's a snap lock to any of the outside doors, so someone—the murderer—could have left it locked behind him?"

"No, I asked. There are only the two outside doors, front and side, and of course the front has that great medieval bar. Primitive, but very effective for all that. The back door—side door—whatever you want to call it—has an old-fashioned lock. You Americans call it a dead bolt, I believe—locks only with a key from either side. So, it looks as though our murderer—if it was murder—had a key."

"Assuming Mrs. Finch was right about the door being locked when she arrived this morning. I'm sure she wasn't lying on purpose, but she might have just assumed it was locked, because it always was."

Alan looked dubious. "An old lock like that is apt to be pretty stiff. I should think there'd be a fairly obvious click or screech when the bolt gave way. Hard to think she'd not notice a difference."

"True." I sat silent for a moment, absently sipping my tea. "Why did you say, 'if it was murder'?"

He shrugged. "Cautious habit, I suppose. They don't know the cause of death yet, of course. It could, stretching the limits of possibility, have been suicide or accident, but Morrison seemed to think the body had been moved to the broom cupboard, which would mean . . ."

I put down my cup, and Alan scraped back his chair.

"It's time we got you to that precious job of yours, if you're still determined to work this afternoon."

We strolled across the Cathedral Close together. Sherebury's Close, a broad area of grass and trees and flower beds surrounding the cathedral, is bordered not only by the administrative buildings of the cathedral and the homes of her clergy, but by a few commercial buildings. Alderney's, at the far end by the west gate, is followed by a bank, a jeweler, a gift shop, and my favorite pub, the Rose and Crown. The Olde English effect makes tourists go into ecstasies, especially on days like today.

The sun glinted off diamond-paned windows and shone warm on our backs. Someone across the Close was cutting the grass, the scent perfuming the air, as did the pink roses blooming profusely by the path. Birds sang in the tops of the oak trees while squirrels chased each other noisily round and round the trunks. Looming benevolently over all, the cathedral dozed in early-afternoon languor, and beyond it, on the other side of the precinct wall, we could just see the uneven gables and chimneys of my Jacobean house. I pointed.

"It does look picturesque, doesn't it?"

"Pure seventeenth century. Are you any closer to being able to bring it into the twentieth?"

I sighed. "Not really; I'm caught in a maze of bureaucracy. To begin with, I can't get anyone started on plans. It's just plumbing and wiring and windows and that kind of thing, but it seems I need a specialist in old buildings. There are only two firms like that left in Sherebury, and they're both so busy I can't get a commitment. Then after I have the plans I have to apply for grants to help with the cost, from the council and English Heritage, and even if I get the money I can't let anyone get started until I get planning permission, and listed building permission as well." I stopped, out of breath.

"That can take forever. When does your lease expire?"

"That's the trouble—end of August. The owner says he's willing to extend it a bit, since I've contracted to buy, pending all the approvals. But he's not being very pleasant about the delay, and I'm afraid he'll sell it out from under me if things go on for too long. I can't even stand to think about having to move. Where would I ever find another wonderful house like that?"

"It's frightfully inconvenient, of course, a really old house. And you do realize it costs the earth to maintain?"

"Yes, I know, but I love it, Alan. I know it isn't an important house—it's small, and nobody famous ever lived there or slept there or hid there while escaping from whatever—but it's important to me. In a way, it's the symbol of everything I love about England, the respect for the past, the fine workmanship . . . and as that loses ground to the shoddy and modern, as England becomes more and more Americanized, I want to cling to my little corner of grace and tradition."

I looked away, embarrassed, but there was more I had to say. "And, you see—it's home. It would have been Frank's and mine, he loved it, too, and now—it's my security blanket, I suppose." I blinked away a tear and Alan took my hand firmly in wordless sympathy. We walked to the cathedral door in silence.

LATE AS I was, I sat in the nave for a few minutes. The great space was filled with light from massive stained-glass windows, shafts of it coloring the dust in the air, rainbow pools of it lying on the cool stone floor. The voices of tourists and guides seemed only to emphasize the essential quiet. Women attending to the flowers shook the fragrance of roses into the air, to mingle with the scent of old stone and the faint, lingering perfume of incense. Somewhere a flute and a choirboy were practicing Handel.

I stood, restored and ready for my job.

When Frank and I first visited England, I was a bit taken aback by the bookshops in all the cathedrals; visions of Jesus chasing the money changers out of the temple sprang to mind. Once I began to appreciate the finances involved, however, I changed my mind. It costs millions of pounds a year to keep these magnificent buildings from falling down. If bookshops can help preserve the cathedrals for their original purpose of inspiring awe and worship, then I'm all for them, especially as the prices are reasonable and most of the labor is donated by overworked volunteers.

So when I began to cast about for something to do in my adopted home, I tried the bookshop, where Mrs. Williamson made me feel not only welcome but much needed.

I waved to her as I entered the shop, and as soon as she could free herself from a cluster of tourists with questions, she hurried to me with furrowed brow.

"Oh, Dorothy, I've been so *worried*! Has something dreadful happened? When the chief constable rang up—"

"No, no, I'm fine," I interrupted. With one eye on the far corner of the shop, where the other volunteer for the afternoon was working at the cash register, I tried to edge toward the staff room. "Just let me put my things away, won't you, and I'll be right out to help. I really am so sorry, Mrs. Williamson, I can see you're busy and I didn't mean to worry you. I—there was a—an accident that I happened to—er—witness. So I had to stick around for a while."

"You weren't hurt!" Her voice rose as the cathedral organist began to practice, and curious eyes turned toward us, including those of the anemic blond cashier.

"No, it was nothing like that." The shop was beginning to empty as the tourists followed the compelling voice of the organ. "I—um—can we talk about it later? I'll just leave my purse—"

But it was too late. The volunteer had dealt with the last purchase and was edging toward us like a nervous cat, pale blue eyes full of apprehension. Clarice Pettifer. Mrs. Archibald Pettifer.

"Oh, whatever happened, Dorothy?" she gasped. "Willie said you were with the police!"

There was no evading it. I had wanted a little time to organize my response before facing Clarice, but the shop had cleared. It was just the three of us. I had no excuse.

I took a deep breath. "Clarice, you'd better come back and sit down."

"Why?" Her voice rose and there were pink spots on her cheeks where her pale color had faded even more, leaving painfully obvious makeup. "What's the matter? It isn't—" her hand flew to her mouth "—it isn't Archie?"

"No, he's—I'm sure he's fine. Do sit down."

Mrs. Williamson, bewildered but cooperative, helped me get her into the staff room and onto a chair.

"Tell me, you must tell me!"

I was going about this very badly. Clarice was a fragile, nervy type. Mention of a dead body even in the abstract would upset her, and with her husband involved, I had hoped to break the news gently. Some hope.

"It's nothing to get upset about, really, but—well, it does concern your husband, in a way." I hurried on, trying not to meet Clarice's red-rimmed eyes.

"It's just that—well, I happened to be in the Town Hall—"

"The Town Hall?" Her voice dropped to a whisper, and her hand moved to her mouth again.

"Yes, I was talking to Mrs. Finch, the cleaning lady, and she happened to—um—" I cast about for a euphemism. There weren't any.

"I'm sorry, but she—we—found a dead man."

We were able to catch Clarice before she hit the floor.

BETWEEN US, WE managed to move her to the shabby couch that, with a dilapidated overstuffed chair, a tiny sink, and an electric kettle, constituted the luxury of the staff room. I bathed her forehead with cool water while Mrs. Williamson ran distractedly into the shop to shoo out two or three browsers and put the "Closed" sign on the door. When she got back, Clarice was beginning to stir.

"I think we'd better have the doctor, don't you?" said Mrs. Williamson. She hugged her midriff; her ulcer must have been giving her fits.

"Oh, no," said Clarice, weakly but quite distinctly. "I'm quite all right, really." She struggled to sit up and went white again. "No, if I could just—rest for a bit— really, I don't want a doctor—Archie wouldn't like—might I have a glass of water, do you think?"

I got the water. "Are you sure you don't need a doctor? You're still terribly pale."

"No."

I recognized in the set of the little rosebud mouth the stubbornness sometimes found in normally compliant people. "Then I'm taking you home. Do you have your car?"

"Oh, no, I'm sure I can manage. We can't leave Willie—the shop—"

"Don't be silly." Mrs. Williamson's voice was suddenly crisp. "You've both—had a shock. If I can't cope alone, I'll recruit some emergency help or leave the shop closed."

It was a noble sacrifice at the height of the tourist season, and I said so. "That's very kind of you, Mrs. Williamson. If I see someone on my way out, I'll—"

"You will not; you've enough to do. I'll see to it. And I do wish you'd call me Willie. You make me feel like your grandmother. Clarice, can you walk?"

It was a long way from the bookshop to the cathedral parking lot, but one of the vergers helped with Clarice. And then Clarice's car turned out to be a BMW, and the thought of driving it on the left side of the narrow Sherebury streets nearly undid me. But Clarice was in no shape to drive and my own sturdy little VW was in my garage, so there was no help for it. I got in the driver's seat and prayed, and somehow we made it without a scratch.

I don't know what kind of house I'd expected the Pettifers to live in. I suppose, knowing they were rich, I'd imagined a stately old manor house of some sort. I couldn't have been more wrong. The house, built at the crest of one of Sherebury's many hills, was certainly close to the million-pound class, but it was brand, spanking new and seemed at a glance to consist mostly of white stone and glass. The entry hall was tiled in black and white; the stairway was marble and chrome—the spotless, sterile home of a wealthy, childless couple.

Over her feeble protests I helped Clarice up to bed in her frilly, feminine bedroom, an interesting contrast to the rest of the house, and then went down to the kitchen to make the universal English cure, a nice cup of tea.

The kitchen, full of all the latest gadgets, was so clean and neat I wondered if Clarice or anyone else ever cooked in it. I took extreme care not to spill anything as I made the tea. Back upstairs, I somewhat guiltily slipped into Clarice's bathroom and explored the medicine chest before I went into the bedroom with the tea.

"I couldn't find any biscuits," I said cheerfully as I set the tray on the bedside table and poured out a cup. "You'd better have a lot of sugar in the tea, though." Not only is sugar good for shock, it would help disguise the taste of the sleeping pill I'd dropped into the cup.

"Oh, I always take four lumps," Clarice said. "Archie says it's a low taste. You're being very kind, Dorothy."

"Don't be silly. How are you feeling?"

"I'm quite all right, really." A tiny bit of color came into her cheeks. "I expect you think I'm a frightful bore, fainting like that."

"Not at all. I should have been more tactful—"

"It was just that—Archie has been spending so much time at the Town Hall, and I was afraid—of course, I realize you'd have told me if . . ." She trailed off and looked at me anxiously.

"Oh, he's fine. He was there, as a matter of fact; he came in just after we—made our discovery."

"When . . . ?"

"Very close to noon."

"Then why didn't he ring me? I was at home until after one. Why hasn't he come home?"

There was panic in her voice again. I did my best.

"The police kept us quite a long time, asking questions, and Mr.—your husband was still there when I left. I expect they wanted to discuss the—er—layout of the building. And so on." And may St. Peter, or whoever keeps an eye on liars, forgive me. "Would you like me to try to find him for you? I don't think you should be alone."

That threw her back into a dither. "Oh—well—he'll be annoyed, if he's busy—but perhaps—I *should* like to talk to him—but if he's doing something important—I don't know, I'm sure—"

"I'll tell you what." She was working herself up again, and I wanted the sedative to take effect. "I'll see if I can track him down, and then he can decide what to do. You finish that tea, and I'll be right back. No, I'll use the phone in the kitchen; it may take several calls and I don't want to disturb you."

Before I left the room, I managed to unplug the phone beside the bed. I had all too good an idea where Archie might be, and I didn't want Clarice to hear.

3

AFTER A FEW anxious minutes, I managed to reach Alan, but it was a few more before he could check with his men and call back with news that wasn't as bad as I'd feared.

"Then they're going to let him go?"

"Oh, yes, certainly, nothing to hold him for. Remember, we're not even certain it's murder, yet. Pettifer's being questioned closely as a matter of routine."

I snorted.

"Oh, heard that one before, have you? Useful phrase, I admit, but in this case it's true. We need statements before people can forget details—or change their stories.

"I did gather Morrison isn't very happy with Pettifer. Apparently Pettifer admits to closing the eyes whilst you and Mrs. Finch were fortifying yourselves. He says he couldn't bear to be stared at by a dead man. Very well, but he had no business to do it, and he probably destroyed valuable evidence. There are also one or two fingerprints that look like friend Archie's, but then, there would be, wouldn't there? He's still in and out of the building rather a lot.

"The problem, of course, is that there are damned few prints, or fibers, or what have you, about the place at all. Mrs. Finch is too efficient, bless her misguided heart. They'll have to talk to the old dear later, ask exactly where she wreaked her havoc."

"They've already asked, and believe me, she won't appreciate repeating it. Alan, what can I tell Clarice? I don't want to break the news that her husband is a murder suspect if I don't have to. She's frantic, and she wants him home. When do you think . . . ?"

"That's up to Morrison, of course, but it may be quite a time yet. They want to grill Pettifer about his alibi. It looks as though our man died before midnight, and Pettifer says he had a dinner meeting with the Lord Mayor and some others early on, and then went drinking with a builder friend, one Herbert Benson. It'll have to be checked."

"Alan, how—do they know how the poor man died?"

"They're theorizing he took a sharp right to the jaw—I don't know if you noticed the bruise—and was knocked into the newel post. It's iron hard after four hundred–odd years; it would have done for him. That doesn't explain, of course, why he was found several yards away behind a closed door. However, Pettifer has no apparent injuries to either hand—and he would have if he'd delivered a blow like that. Which is another good reason to let him go.

"At any rate, he'll be released presently, I suspect in rather a foul mood. I gather we haven't treated him with quite the deference he seems to feel is his due." Alan's voice held a hint of a chuckle.

I was not amused. "Oh, fine, an irate husband is just what Clarice needs. That man mustn't be allowed to bully her when he gets home, and I certainly can't referee between them. He and I get along like two strange cats; I'd be worse than no help at all."

I heard a faint sigh. Alan needed to get back to his own affairs, but his manners held. "What about Mrs. Finch?"

"What about her?"

"Why don't you ring her up? She strikes me as the motherly type when she's not having hysterics. Would she, perhaps, enjoy ministering to Clarice?"

"Alan, you're a genius! Ada Finch is the very person. Pettifer's used to having her around, and she'll adore being in the middle of things. I'll call her right now, and you can get back to worrying about the Prince."

After three tries I hit the right Mrs. Finch, and she was there in ten minutes, talking a blue streak. We went upstairs to find Clarice still awake and fretting.

"Clarice, do you know Mrs. Finch? She works for the city and knows Mr. Pettifer, and she's come to stay with you for a while, at least until he gets home. I wasn't able to speak to him, but I gather he'll be out for a bit longer, and I didn't like to leave you alone." I was rather pleased with my little speech and its careful omissions, but Mrs. Finch opened her mouth and nearly spoiled everything.

"And 'oo better than me to look after you, as can understand wot you're goin' through, me 'avin' a 'usband as was never 'ome when I needed 'im, though with 'im it was the drink, not bein' mixed up with—"

I shook my head frantically and Mrs. Finch went on without missing a beat, "—with important affairs like your man. But there, a man's a man when all's said an' done and the best of 'em can't 'old a candle to a woman when things 'as come crashin' down about our 'eads. Now, dearie, just you stay right there an' 'ave yourself a nice lie down. It'll do you a power o' good, an' you're not to worry about a thing, I'll see to it all."

The tide of words flowed over Clarice like syrup, completing the work the pill had begun. She relaxed back into her pillows with a little sigh, like a child. Probably, I thought, she'd had a nanny just like Mrs. Finch.

"Thank you so much, Mrs. Finch." Her voice was weak, but

she almost smiled. "I'm quite all right, really, but it's very kind of you to stay if you can spare the time. It was clever of you to think of this, Dorothy."

I would pass on the thanks; now was not the time to give credit where credit was due. Clarice's eyes were closing; her hands lay trustingly half open. She looked very young; for the first time I wondered just how much older her husband was. Mrs. Finch put a finger to her lips and, tiptoeing heavily, drew me out of the room.

It was getting on toward suppertime, but if I wanted to talk to Mrs. Finch, I knew I was doomed to a nice cup of tea. We headed for the kitchen, where she put the kettle on and found another teapot while I sat and appraised the room.

Mr. Pettifer had certainly done well for himself. After all the window-shopping I'd been slogging through, planning the improvements I wanted to make to my own house, I had a pretty good idea just how many thousands of pounds a kitchen like this would cost. Everything was the very best, though the decor was peculiarly mixed. White cabinets, white tile countertops, white appliances made for a hospital-like sterility, but the bright curtains and canisters, the hooked rugs, the lovely old Welsh dresser with flowery china displayed on its shelves looked like a very different personality at work. Perhaps Clarice did have some say in her household, after all.

"Naow, then!" Mrs. Finch plunked the tea tray in the middle of the kitchen table, sat down, and got right to the point. " 'Oo do you think done it?"

I recalled my thoughts abruptly. "Well, actually, I—"

"I think it was 'im." Her eyes rolled upward, presumably to the bedroom above. " 'Er 'usband. Mr. Bleedin' Muckety-Muck."

"He has an alibi," I said before I remembered that the information was probably confidential.

Mrs. Finch shrugged away an alibi with fine disdain. " 'Ee would 'ave, wouldn't 'ee? They always do."

I realized I was dealing with a fellow lover of detective fiction. "Well, there is that," I admitted. "But, Mrs. Finch, why do you think he did it? I mean, not just why do you think so, but what motive would he have had? We don't even know who the victim is, yet."

"So 'ow would I know why 'ee done it?" She waved her hand airily. " 'Ee got in 'is way."

The pronouns were a little ambiguous, but I understood that she meant the victim somehow inconvenienced Pettifer.

"But wot I mean to say is, 'oo else would it be? 'Ee was in and out o' the place every time you turned around, doin' 'oo knows wot. *And* 'ee still had a key, and wot for, I'd like to know?"

"You know, I wondered that myself. Was he planning his new project, measuring and so on?" It sounded thin, even to me, and Mrs. Finch gave me her best pitying look.

" 'Ee don't do that 'imself, dearie," she said, as to a not too bright child. " 'Ee's got architects and 'oo knows wot to do all the work. And they've been traipsin' through as well, trackin' mud all over me clean floors and talkin' about 'ow they was gonner pull down this and build over that till I could've 'it 'em over the 'ead wiv me mop.

"Wot I think," she said, lowering her voice and gesturing once more toward the ceiling, "I think 'ee was meetin' some woman there. And the more shame to 'im, with 'is pore wife sittin' at 'ome, cryin' 'er 'eart out—"

"You don't have to whisper; I gave Mrs. Pettifer a sleeping pill and I think she's out for the count. But, Mrs. Finch, think what you're saying! Not that I'd put it past him, but in the Town Hall? There's not a stick of furniture in the place. Where would they—I mean—?"

She laughed richly. "It don't want thinkin' about, do it? Ah, well, there you 'as me. But this I do know, an' I'll 'old to, as 'ee was plottin' somethin', wot I don't know, sneakin' about an' jumpin' a foot if I comes near. Asks me wot I was doin' there.

Wot *I* was doin' there, if you please, when I was only doin' me job wot I get paid for, same as I've always done, and no thanks for it, neither. Wot was *'ee* doin' there, I'd like to know?"

That seemed to get us back to where we'd started. "What *I'd* like to know, Mrs. Finch—" I began, when she put her finger to her lips with an exaggerated gesture. A car door slammed. A key turned in the front door.

With a conspiratorial grin, Mrs. Finch gestured frantically toward the back door.

"I'll call you!" I mouthed, gathered up my belongings, and got out before my dignity got caught in the door.

THE FIRST ORDER of business, when I'd managed the long walk home, was, of course, to feed the cats—cats have a way of making sure they always come first. Once they'd settled down happily to a dish of liver and bacon, I was free to think about my own belated meal.

The knock at the back door came while I was still standing in front of the open refrigerator.

"Come in, Jane." I closed the fridge and opened the cupboard. "I'm just trying to find something to eat in this house. All I seem to have is cat food and noodles, and I'm not sure a Seafood Treat casserole sounds appealing."

"Thought you'd be in no mood to cook, after the day you've had. Does cold roast beef sound good?"

"Heavenly! You're a lifesaver. I wanted to talk to you anyway."

I didn't question how she knew about my day. It had taken me only a few weeks of living in Sherebury to understand that there is very little privacy in a cathedral town. Some mysterious equivalent of jungle drums ensures that everyone will know everyone else's business, at least within cathedral circles. Jane, a retired teacher with friends all over town, knows everything that happens in Sherebury, including what is likely to happen and what is reputed to have happened but didn't. It makes her a marvelous source of information for an outsider like me.

I trailed happily after her across the backyard.

She waited with commendable patience until we were established in her kitchen with lovely thin slices of rare beef, fragrant crusty bread, and a horseradish sauce guaranteed to clear up any sinus condition. Along with mugs of beer, mine frosty-cold for my peculiar American taste. Jane is truly a paragon.

"Tell me about Clarice Pettifer," I said finally, after I'd taken a couple of bites of my superb sandwich and shooed away three amiably slobbering bulldogs whose eyes were alight with hope.

"Worm," said Jane. "Spineless. Wouldn't say boo to a goose. Not," she added, "that I've ever known what good it would do a person to say boo to a goose. However. Lived in Sherebury all her life, pretty when she was young, chocolate-box type. Enough, dogs! Go!"

They retreated a few inches and I pursued the subject. "Really! I would never have guessed. I can see it now that you mention it, though, the fair skin and china-blue eyes and so on. I suppose that's what attracted Pettifer."

Jane snorted and went on with her story. "Father well-off, owned ironmongers' shops all over the county. Started converting them to DIY shops just before the craze for do-it-yourself set in, made a fortune."

"Oh, she isn't from a—an old family—that is . . ." I floundered.

Jane barked one of her disconcerting laughs. "What you mean is, is she upper class? Never know why Americans get so embarrassed about it. No, she isn't. Common as good English dirt, her family was, and not ashamed of it. She'd have turned out sensible if they'd lived."

"What happened?"

"Killed in an accident when Clarice was only seventeen, both her father and mother. She was left a rich orphan."

"Oh, dear. And Pettifer?" I asked, guessing the rest of the scenario.

"He was working for her father, or with him. Twelve years older than she is, you know. Involved in building the new shops. Saw a chance to rake in a fortune and a pretty wife at one go. Swept her off her feet." Jane's tone was dry enough to dehumidify a swamp. "They married when she was eighteen."

"So the money in the family is hers."

"Not all of it. Give the devil his due, he's worked hard, made a fortune of his own. Best builder in town."

"You keep surprising me. I thought he was just a developer, a—a monument-gobbling monster."

"Now, perhaps. Not back then, before he fell in love with money and power."

There was a dismal little silence.

"What a depressing story," I said finally, finishing my beer. "So that was how long ago, when they were married, I mean? Thirty years or so?"

"Twenty, more like." At the look on my face, Jane laughed, without amusement. "They're both younger than they look. He cultivates the pompous role. That's why you thought she was a nob. He's bullied her into the proper accent and the proper clothes and the proper charities till she's washed out and dried up before her time. Bloody bastard."

I raised my eyebrows. Jane is plainspoken, but seldom coarse. A horrid thought crossed my mind.

"Is he—you don't think he actually beats her? I've never seen any bruises, but . . ."

"Not that kind of bastard. Browbeats her, ignores her, sucks all the life out of her and then despises her for being dull and dead. More beer?"

"Thanks." I held out my pewter mug. "You know, though,

I've always thought that people who act like doormats positively invite other people to walk on them.'"

"Something in that," Jane acknowledged. "Adoration brings out the worst in some men. No excuse, though."

"No." I laughed, a little bitterly. "I thought, today, that she responded so well to Mrs. Finch because she'd had a nanny like her. And all the time—"

"She *is* Mrs. Finch, that's the answer. Only without the sense. Now, Dorothy, tell me. All I know is, Ada Finch found a murdered man."

"Well—a body anyway," I said, and proceeded to tell her all I knew. "And I was just getting around to asking Mrs. Finch exactly what she'd seen this morning, when Pettifer—I cannot bring myself to call that man 'Archie'—came home and I beat it out of there. Do you suppose she's right about him being a womanizer?"

"There are rumors," Jane said. "But not at the Town Hall, not even for a meeting place."

"No," I agreed with a yawn. "Too cautious." I yawned again and put my plate on the floor to be snuffled over by the dogs, who had crept back to the table. "So if I want to soothe Clarice's fears, what do you think I ought to do next?"

"Go home to bed," said Jane promptly. "You were up with the lark. Tomorrow's soon enough to start asking awkward questions. And Alan will have some ideas of his own."

"He's going to be too busy with the royal visit to do much about this one, I think. Which is fine with me—it means I can poke around with no interference."

"Except possibly from the murderer," said Jane.

4

THAT EVENTFUL DAY was a Monday. The next day, Tuesday, normal English summer weather reasserted itself. The soothing, steady patter of rain on my roof kept me in bed until the cats decided breakfast had been delayed long enough.

I'm ashamed to say that, when my bare foot encountered a puddle on my way to the bathroom, my first reaction was to glare at the cats, who were twining themselves eagerly around my ankles. "All right, which of you was it?" They looked offended (an expression that comes naturally to any cat), and then I felt the drop of water on my head. Outside wasn't the only place it was raining.

So that, by the time I had fed my tyrants and myself, dressed in proper summer clothing (wool sweater and skirt), and put a bucket under the leak, I was in no sweet mood. I'd called my landlord's answering machine with little hope of a prompt response. Though keeping the roof in repair was clearly his responsibility, he'd been dodging my calls for some time, hoping I'd take the house off his hands soon. Well, I was doing all I could, dammit! Muttering to myself, I splashed across the Close to the bookshop.

Mrs. Williamson was puttering about the shop, replacing

stock, dusting a shelf of poetry that was seldom touched. "Good morning, Dorothy. Frightful morning, actually, isn't it? We shan't have many customers today, I shouldn't think. Now tell me, how is poor Clarice? I couldn't quite make out just what sent her into such a tizz."

"I'm not sure myself, but I think she was afraid her husband was going to get into trouble. I left her in Mrs. Finch's capable hands—d'you know Mrs. Finch?" She nodded. "Anyway, Clarice was very shaky when I last saw her. Have you heard from her this morning?"

"Mr. Pettifer rang up last evening to say she wouldn't be in, so I arranged for a substitute, though with the weather what it is, I doubt she'll be needed."

"Well, I'd better hang these things up before I drip all over the stock, and then we'll see what there is to do."

As I put my yellow slicker and hat on the peg in the staff room, Barbara Dean sailed in and my heart sank.

I don't know if Mrs. Dean (she's another one I don't dare call by her first name) set out deliberately to imitate Margaret Thatcher, or if they're just naturally sisters under the skin, but I do know that if Lady Thatcher ever wants a double she need look no farther than Sherebury. The resemblance extends far beyond the helmet of gray-blond hair, the rigid carriage, the steely eye; I haven't the slightest doubt Barbara Dean could run the country quite as efficiently as she runs the Sherebury Preservation Society and several other worthy organizations. She can be utterly charming when she wants to, but her ruthless capability reduces me to quivering jelly.

"Good gracious, Mrs. Martin, you are wet, aren't you?" She looked pointedly at the puddle forming under my slicker.

"Oh, dear, I suppose I should mop that up." And why couldn't I say that being wet is a normal consequence of being out in the rain? Perhaps it was because she appeared to be only a bit damp around the edges. Typical.

"And how is your planning application coming along?" she inquired, shooting her perfectly furled umbrella into the stand. "I assume you are nearly ready to submit it?" She sits on the City Council, naturally, and its Planning Committee.

"Well, no, actually, I can't seem to get anyone to come and talk about what I want to do. And now the roof is leaking, and—"

"Oh, but that can't be allowed." I knew she'd blame me. "You must deal with that at once, mustn't you, or there will be structural damage." It was her best headmistress tone.

"Yes, but I *can't* deal with it." Frustration bubbled over and I dared argue. "I don't own the house yet, so it's still the landlord's responsibility—and he's avoiding me because he hopes I'll be taking over soon. But until I get planning permission— *and* listed building permission—"

"No, no." She waved her hands impatiently. "Simply to repair a roof you need neither, so long as the appearance isn't altered, of course. And you needn't consider your landlord. He is obliged to maintain a listed building; if he avoids his obligations, he can be made to comply. No, your real difficulty lies with the contractors, apparently, who refuse to provide you with plans and an estimate."

"Well, it isn't exactly that they refuse, they just haven't gotten around to—"

"Quite. Obviously you must find someone else."

"There isn't anyone else. I've checked with every—"

"Nonsense. There's always someone, if one looks in the right place. I shall ask the secretary of Planning Aid to phone you this afternoon; I'm sure she'll be of help."

Planning Aid, the voluntary bureau that is supposed to help steer applicants through the maze of the planning system, had been of remarkably little help so far. Of course, Barbara Dean hadn't been the one asking.

"Thank you. I hope—"

"You must move quickly, of course, with respect to the roof, but as for the major renovations, as soon as you have plans I shall present them personally to the committee, and I think I can promise you will have your permission in short order." Another small frown appeared. "The committee has been rather taken up with other matters, to be sure. Mr. Pettifer must be stopped from despoiling the Town Hall. I was rather in despair about it two days ago, I don't mind admitting. However," she coughed delicately, "er—current events have rather rendered the issue moot, for the moment."

I was visited by sudden inspiration. "Things went Mr. Pettifer's way at the Lord Mayor's meeting, then?"

She looked at me sharply, but didn't ask how I knew about the meeting. "Certainly the prevailing wind seemed to be blowing his way, discounting a few—er—personalities that were exchanged. However, that was only a small and hardly a disinterested group of people. If you are at all concerned about the Town Hall, I suggest you attend the public meeting this evening, where the matter will be thoroughly aired. Seven o'clock, in the Victoria Hall."

The Victoria Hall, designed for concerts, was the largest meeting place in Sherebury outside the cathedral. They must be expecting a crowd.

"I'm very interested in the fate of the Town Hall. I'll be there."

I'd actually been allowed to complete a few sentences, I reflected as we went into the shop to deal with an unexpected busload of Japanese tourists. I was making progress.

I was also intrigued about what manner of "personalities" might have been exchanged Sunday night. In the mouth of a Barbara Dean, the phrase might mean anything from a nasty glare to fisticuffs. She allowed me no opening to ask, however, and, in fact, spoke to me only once more, just before lunch.

"I assume that you will be at home early this afternoon, Mrs. Martin? So that Planning Aid can ring you?"

It was obviously a royal command. I nodded humbly; it was all I could do not to tug my forelock.

The Planning Aid secretary, when she called about two-thirty, was much more approachable.

"Mrs. Dean asked me to ring you first thing this afternoon; I'm sorry I'm a bit late, but it took a little time to find the information you need. I did manage to reach Mr. Peabody—he's the local chairman for listed building permission. He said you don't need an architect just for the roof; roof repairs aren't tricky so long as the proper materials are used. Any good builder will do, and there's a new one in town you might try. He says he knows nothing about the man at all, but as he's new, he might not be booked up. Do you have a pencil? Right, then his name is Herbert Benson and his number is Sherebury 43527. I do hope it'll work out."

Her warm concern was an agreeable change. If I owed it to Barbara Dean, I was duly grateful.

Now. Herbert Benson. The name sounded vaguely familiar, with some slightly unpleasant association. I teased my brain for a moment, but whatever it was just buried itself deeper, so I made the phone call. I didn't have a lot of choice.

The man sounded nice enough and promised to come look at the roof on Thursday. I enjoyed leaving another message for the invisible landlord, informing him of his obligation in the matter of roof repairs, and set off for the Town Hall meeting a few hours later with a spring in my step.

I'd decided to walk, even though it was a stiffish pull to the university. The rain had let up a little, and I told myself parking would be impossible to find. My hat, quite a modest affair this time in pale-pink straw with a simple white ribbon, would be amply protected by my umbrella, and my shoes didn't matter. I refused to admit, even to myself, my fear of driving in a country where they use the wrong side of the road and consider roundabouts to be the ideal intersection control. Myself, I find them indistinguishable from Dante's circles of hell.

Cowardice or not, walking turned out to be a smart move. The parking lots really were jammed by the time I got there, and hardly any seats were left in the Victoria Hall, even though extra chairs had been set up in the back. I secured one of them, glad to sit down even on a folding wooden chair, settled my hat, and studied with interest the people milling around the great, uncomfortable box of a room. The floor sloped sharply toward the stage, so from my position behind the last row of theater-style seats I could see everyone, the backs of their heads if nothing else.

It was a strangely mixed crowd. The chattering classes were prominent. The women, dressed with what looked like an almost deliberate lack of chic, fiddled with their pearls and conversed in throttled, well-bred voices. Mine, as usual, was the only hat in evidence. The men, in rumpled tweed suits, looked as though they wished they could smoke the pipes that bulged in their pockets.

The other distinct element, sitting in a solid block and looking somewhat formidable, consisted of working-class men and a few women. Some of the men on the other side of the hall, the ones in suits, were eyeing the workers uneasily, and I, too, hoped that feelings wouldn't run too high for civilized discussion. I settled back into my chair with some apprehension as the Lord Mayor walked onto the stage, chain of office and all, and everyone took their seats. This meeting was going to be interesting, at the very least.

The Lord Mayor was followed by Barbara Dean and Archibald Pettifer, who sat down, avoiding each other's eyes, as the Lord Mayor moved up to the lectern.

He cleared his throat. "Ladies and gentlemen, if I may have your attention, please . . . ah, thank you. I think we are ready to begin.

"As you all know, we in Sherebury have for some time been quite concerned about the fate of our Town Hall. It has, most regrettably, been allowed to fall into a state of disrepair owing to the lack of funds to restore it. Although grants have been sought, some of you may know that the final resort to English Heritage was unsuccessful; the cost of necessary repairs is estimated to run to millions of pounds, and since the Council simply cannot provide the city's share, English Heritage have declined their help.

"This decision, rendered only in the past few days, has been a major blow to preservation efforts. However, as you may also know, an alternative proposal has been on the table for some time. This proposal, put forward by Mr. Pettifer—" the mayor nodded gravely to Pettifer, who nodded back "— is, briefly, that he use his own funds to restore the Town Hall, in several stages, in return for which he would be granted a ninety-nine-year lease on the building. There is, of course, a quid pro quo: The proposal is contingent upon his being allowed to effect certain nonstructural changes to the interior of the building so that he could put it to commercial use."

There was a murmur at that, soft but menacing, and I saw Barbara Dean's hands, clasped in her lap, make a convulsive little movement before she controlled them.

"Ah, I see that many of you are familiar with Mr. Pettifer's plans," said the mayor with just the hint of a smile. It was exactly the right touch; a chuckle passed lightly through the room and the tension dissipated—for the moment.

"Because the Town Hall decision is a matter so controversial, and so fundamental to the city, the chairman of the Planning Committee has invited me as your lord mayor to take the chair of this meeting. I have invited Mr. Pettifer, and Mrs. Dean, chairman of the Sherebury Preservation Society, to present their views on the matter. I think I may safely say that those views have points of difference."

Again the crowd chuckled. I began to see why this man was such a successful politician.

"After their formal remarks, I shall open the floor for discussion. I ask those who wish to speak to come to one of the microphones, identify themselves, and keep their remarks brief, so that we may allow everyone a chance.

"Mr. Pettifer, will you begin?"

Pettifer, as he took the mayor's place at the lectern, cut rather a poor figure by contrast. Although the mayor's suit was older and his hair thinner, his tall, spare figure and ascetic face held a dignity that made his elaborate chain of office seem a natural part of his ensemble. Pettifer's tailoring was impeccable, his shoes were polished to a high gloss, but there was nothing he could do about a florid complexion or a tendency to embonpoint. I was reminded of a Kewpie doll trying to be impressive, and suddenly, most unexpectedly, I felt a little sorry for him.

"My friends," he said in the unctuous tones that had doubtless won him votes over the years, "I see no need to belabor the points our esteemed lord mayor has made so eloquently. The facts are very clear indeed. Our Town Hall is falling down. Although the exterior walls remain sound, the roof and the interior are in sorry condition. I am fully prepared to present the reports of the inspectors should you wish to take the time, but there is no disagreement about their verdict. If the necessary repairs are not made, and made soon, this precious monument to Sherebury's illustrious history will be lost forever.

"You will note that I have referred to the exalted status of the building in order to take the words out of the mouth of my distinguished opponent." He bowed and smiled at Barbara Dean as the crowd tittered; her smile in return was a mere baring of teeth.

"My friends, I am a builder by trade. I would venture to say that no one—I repeat, no one—in Sherebury is more aware than I of the great beauty and exemplary workmanship represented by the Town Hall. I revere its builders as the geniuses they were. BUT!"

He raised an admonitory finger. "As I venerate the building, so I am convinced that it is a living building, deserving, and indeed requiring, to be of use. Did its builders intend it to be an object of worship? No! They constructed it for use, use by the journeymen of the town of Sherebury, by ordinary people like you and me."

He looked directly at the group of workmen, who responded with nods and nudgings and one muted cry of " 'Ear, 'ear!" from a walrus-mustached man standing against the wall.

Encouraged, Pettifer leaned forward and rested his forearms on the lectern. "Now, we all know that Sherebury is in economic trouble. Hundreds of able-bodied men in our small community are unable to find work; hundreds more have left with their wives and families to seek a better life elsewhere. Can we afford to let this situation continue? Can we afford to allow our strongest and best workers to remain in despair, or depart in disgust? My friends, I say we cannot, and I have a solution. Put them to work on the Town Hall! Bring new business to town, new commerce in my Town Hall Mall. Rescue, not just a fine building, but the spirit of Sherebury!"

The rising murmurs of approval from the workmen erupted in a little chorus of cheers. The rest of the room sat in chilly silence as Pettifer sat down and Barbara Dean stepped forward, every silver hair lacquered into place, every line of her powder blue suit firmly under control.

"You're quite a powerful speaker, sir," she said with a ferocious smile. "I wonder you don't go into Parliament." The quote from Dickens was a nasty little dig at Pettifer's political ambitions. His face turned puce as he bowed coldly.

"I am sure, however, that your audience is too intelligent to be swayed by political posturings. Let us return to our senses, ladies and gentlemen, from which we have been invited to take leave, and consider. Mr. Pettifer pretends that he has two motives, both philanthropic: He wishes to preserve the fabric of the Town Hall and he wishes to assume the role of Father Christmas to the workingmen of Sherebury. I submit that, although he does bear some physical resemblance—" she stared meaningfully at Pettifer's little paunch and raised a giggle or two "—his essential characteristic is more Scroogelike.

"We are all heartily sick and tired of militaristic governments throughout the world who for so many years have insisted that the way to preserve the peace is by making war. I submit that Mr. Pettifer's plan to preserve the Town Hall by despoiling it falls into the same category of logic. I submit that those workmen whom he is so anxious to protect could be as fully employed in the proper restoration of the Town Hall as in its desecration.

"Can anyone doubt that Mr. Pettifer's real motives are much simpler? Profit and personal aggrandizement are far more likely to drive such a man than philanthropy. I would ask you to consider Mr. Pettifer's plans, of which most of you are aware, to build what he refers to as 'University Housing.' He has sought planning permission to pull down a row of perfectly sound houses which rent cheaply—to students, for the most part—and put up cracker boxes in their stead. Can we doubt that the rents will be far higher? Can we doubt that the profits will be far higher than if the existing houses were simply renovated?

"This is the man who asks you to give the Town Hall into his hands. I ask you all: Is there anyone here who can point to any action in Mr. Pettifer's past that shows his concern for the public good? Is he a notable contributor to any charity? Has he, in fact, ever given a shilling to the poor or even rescued a stray dog?"

The murmurs had been growing, and now one workman spoke loudly enough to be heard. "Sacked me once, 'ee did, for nothin' at all!" The mood of the crowd had changed, as is the fickle way of crowds. As the level of sound in the room rose and took on an ugly undertone, I felt a moment of panic. Was this meeting going to degenerate into a riot?

5

"NOW, LADIES AND gentlemen." Mrs. Dean raised her hands in placatory fashion, and spoke in tones that were honeyed, clear, and low enough that people were forced to hush in order to hear her. Clever, I thought. The workmen sat down again.

"You must not think that I wish to assassinate Mr. Pettifer's character." Chuckles and a couple of jeers. "No, indeed. If that were my purpose, I have more serviceable weapons at my command." More laughter, with a mean-tempered edge to it. I thought for a moment that she was going to refer to the murder, and Pettifer looked up sharply, but Dean was apparently not prepared to stoop so low. Or maybe she thought the insinuation was sufficient.

She went on. "I am simply trying to impress upon you that he is not the man we need for the job at hand, which is to save the Town Hall. I have a plan, ladies and gentlemen, and I ask you to listen carefully and—without prejudice—decide whether it is not a better plan for the purpose."

The languid majority sat up and perked their ears.

"Until now we have put our faith in grants from outside

Sherebury. As the Lord Mayor has told you, all these appeals have come to naught. It is time to look to our own community, time to take our fate into our own hands. I have, therefore, in the past several days, had conversations with the leaders of Sherebury: political, religious, commercial, and educational. Everyone was most eager to cooperate in a massive fund drive for the preservation of one of Sherebury's most important pieces of history. To be specific: Our lord mayor, Councillor Daniel Clarke, has agreed to open his home for a fête in aid of the cause. The Very Reverend Mr. Kenneth Allenby, Dean of the Cathedral, proposed that one night of the forthcoming Cathedral Music Festival be dedicated to the Town Hall, with all proceeds being donated to the fund. A number of businessmen and -women have agreed to allow solicitation of funds at their places of business, and many have promised personal or corporate donations, as well. And finally, the vice chancellor of Sherebury University has agreed to enlist the aid of a number of students, not only as solicitors, but in the planning of benefit projects.

"Ladies and gentlemen, if this much support can be generated in a few days, is there any question that we can raise our share of the necessary funds? We must prove to English Heritage that Sherebury has the will to save the Town Hall. We must do it, and we shall!"

The crowd was with her now. Cheers and shouts of "Hear, hear!" sounded from all sides. As the Lord Mayor began to restore order, rapping on the lectern, and the people resumed their seats, one woman rose from her seat on the aisle and marched to the nearest microphone. I recognized her after a moment as the owner of a gift shop in the High Street. She was dressed in a bright yellow suit, somewhat too tight, and her fiercely red hair positively bristled. She raised her voice.

"Lord Mayor, may I speak?"

"Certainly, certainly, everyone must have a chance to be heard—if you will please be seated—your attention, please!"

The woman at the microphone began to speak before all the noise had abated, but her angry tones cut through.

"And what about me, I'd like to know? Me and all the other shopkeepers in town? Where do we fit into this lovely scheme? It's all very well to save a building, but what's the point if there's nobody to use it?"

The Mayor interrupted her. "For the record, will you identify yourself, please?"

"Mavis Underwood, as you know. I keep the gift shop in the High Street, and three more in Seldon, Watsford, and King's Abbot, and you all know that, too. *And* you know how business is in Sherebury High Street. Or if you don't, I'll tell you. It scarcely exists. This month my receipts won't meet my rent, and not for the first time, and the other merchants will tell you the same. How much longer can we operate at a loss?" There was a little murmur of agreement from various quarters of the room.

"At the end of the day, the Sherebury shop is an albatross, dragging the rest down. I need—we all need—new clientele, and a new mall will bring them. The Town Hall Mall—that's different than the rest; it'll draw the punters. What'll an empty building draw? Flies!"

She took a deep breath, audible over the sound system, and was clearly prepared to go on in the same vein, but the Lord Mayor cut her off neatly.

"Thank you so much, Mrs. Underwood. Your point of view is a valuable one, which I'm sure represents the thoughts of many here." He turned toward a microphone on the other side of the room. "Mr. Farrell, have you something to say?"

"William Farrell, contractor." He spoke in a deep growl that boomed out over the loudspeakers and set up an excruciating shriek of feedback. While someone tried to adjust the volume, I studied the man with interest. He was standing at a microphone near the back of the room, and although I couldn't see most of his face, I could see the tension in his prominent jaw. He was altogether a formidable-looking person, tall and powerfully built, with dark hair and a hulking sort of squareness to his shoulders that reminded me uncomfortably of Boris Karloff.

"I'm so sorry, Mr. Farrell," said the Lord Mayor. "Would you like to try again?"

"What I've got to say is soon said. There's no need for all this talk. I've had a proposal on the table for nearly a year now to build a proper mall, with proper parking and access, at the old hop farm on the A28. There's your new clientele, Mavis. There's your traffic; you all know how much traffic the A28 carries every day of the week. No need to put the Town Hall to a silly use that was never intended. Preserve it; take the shopping out of town, where people want it nowadays. Everyone's pleased."

Mr. Pettifer didn't look pleased at all, and jumped up to reply, but the Lord Mayor motioned to him with a frown, and he sat down, folding his arms across his chest, the alarming color rising again in his face.

There was a stirring in the group of workmen and then a middle-aged man with sparse gray hair, evidently chosen as their spokesman, forced his way out of a tightly packed row of seats and moved to the microphone.

"I'm Jem 'Iggins, Yer Worship," he said, grasping the mike stand uneasily in gnarled hands. "And like a lot of us 'ere tonight, I'm out of work. And what me mates and me got ter say is, we don't none of us care where they builds whatever they're goin' to build, so long as we 'as a part in it. But it 'pears to us as if the work would be double, like, if they was to do them repairs to the Town Hall *and* build their shoppin' mall someplace else. And it stands to reason, don't it, that if we 'as more money, we'll spend more money, and that's good for trade, too. And—that's all."

He turned away abruptly to an approving chorus from his mates, and now everyone was eager to speak. A few malcontents grumbled about various aspects of the problem, and a few more wandered far from the issue at hand, arguing about everything from civic government in general to environmental issues to animal rights, but most of the comments reiterated support for Mrs. Dean's preservation efforts, and the audience grew restive.

I stopped listening and concentrated on watching Pettifer. His color had returned to its normal hue, but his expression had set in a hard half smile. He had lost this battle, and he knew it, but he hadn't given up the war. Too good a politician to try to sway a crowd that had so obviously turned against him, he nevertheless sat erect in his chair, looking each speaker defiantly in the eye. Some of them faltered in mid-speech, and Pettifer looked grimly satisfied each time.

Finally the Lord Mayor decided to call a halt. "Thank you, ladies and gentlemen. I think we have been able to air this matter thoroughly, and I thank you for your time and patience, and for your courtesy in listening to other points of view. You understand, of course, that as the Town Hall is a Grade I listed building, the Secretary of State will make the ultimate decision about its fate, but you may be sure he will have a report of this meeting. I notice, Mr. Thorpe, that you have made no contribution, and wonder if there is anything you would like to say to close the meeting."

A bulky sort of man got up and moved back a row or two to the nearest mike, a used-car salesman smile on his face. "I have nothing to add, Lord Mayor. My name, for the record, is John Thorpe, and I am an estate agent." He said it as John Gielgud might have said "I am an actor."

"I feel it would be inappropriate for me to comment, since I am likely to be an interested party in dealing with leases for any new mall. I'm sure that all plans put forward today have merit, and simply wish to say, may the best man—or woman—" he sketched a little bow to Mrs. Dean "—win!" He turned away without looking at Pettifer, who was glaring balefully.

"Very well, then, ladies and gentlemen, I thank you all again and declare this meeting adjourned."

I creaked to my feet, stumbling a little. A steadying hand caught my elbow.

"Alan! Bless you, I thought my joints were going to give out on me altogether. My bones do not appreciate two hours of this kind of chair. What are you doing here? I didn't see you when I came in."

"No, I drifted in late. I like to keep my finger on the community pulse, you know, especially when it's getting a trifle feverish—to mix a metaphor. What did you think of the meeting?"

I shivered a little. "It's very different from this sort of thing in America, of course. We'd have everybody yelling at each other. This was all very polite, but it was that terrible English politeness that can feel like being slammed into a meat locker. To tell the truth, it scared me a little. I can see why you're worried. Those workmen were ready to do something drastic, if Barbara Dean hadn't handled them so well—did you get here in time for that?"

Alan nodded. "Played them like a violin, didn't she? Stirring them up to a nice crescendo and then calming them down. A remarkable lady, our Barbara."

I shivered again. "And that Mr. Farrell scares me."

Alan hugged my shoulders. "You've been watching too many old horror videos, is your trouble. How about a drink to take the bogeyman away?"

"And a sandwich—I feel in need of sustenance. Alan, Mr. Pettifer isn't going to take this sitting down, I could tell. He was ready to kill that man Thorpe."

Alan just looked at me and I grimaced.

"Sorry—poor choice of words. But honestly, if looks could kill, I should think you'd have another corpse on your hands. I suppose Thorpe's been in Pettifer's camp and now Pettifer thinks he's a Judas."

"Probably. Where's your car? I didn't ask my driver to wait."

"Then we're out of luck. I walked. For the exercise," I added defiantly.

"One of these days I'm going to make you a present of driving lessons," said Alan cheerfully, looking around. "Ah, constable!"

The uniformed man just leaving the hall stopped in his tracks, trotted over, and saluted smartly, looking anxious. "Yes, sir!"

"It's all right, Wilkins," Alan said, reading the name tag without missing a beat. "I simply need a favor, if you have your car."

Wilkins nodded, mute in the presence of his Big Boss.

"The lady and I need a ride over to the Cathedral Close, if it's not too much trouble."

"Yes, sir. That is, no, sir, no trouble at all, sir. This way, sir—madam."

So we ended the evening peaceably at the Rose and Crown discussing leaky roofs and other domestic disasters, with not a word about murders or civic passions.

OVER BREAKFAST THE next day my mind reverted to the meeting of the night before. I wished I understood a little more about all the crosscurrents. Why, for example, had Thorpe done what looked like such an abrupt about-face? Why hadn't Farrell's proposal—which sounded so reasonable—gained approval, or even discussion, over the past year?

And most of all, what had gone on at that meeting the Lord Mayor had held Sunday night? The tensions at the public meeting had been only thinly veiled; I could well believe in those heated private exchanges Barbara Dean had hinted at.

I considered my sources of information. Jane, of course, but Jane wasn't available at the moment; she volunteered at the animal shelter on Wednesdays. Margaret Allenby, wife of the dean of the cathedral, could sometimes be persuaded to talk about personalities in ecclesiastical circles, and Jeremy Sayers, the organist, was always open to gossip, the bitchier the better—but this wasn't a church matter. It wasn't a university matter, either, which left out dear old Dr. Temple, who knew everything about everyone academic, but wasn't interested in general gossip.

That just about exhausted the possibilities in my limited group of friends, which meant I'd have to wait till Jane got home. Meanwhile, there were other worries to deal with, the foremost being Clarice. Archie couldn't have been feeling very pleasant when he got home last night after the meeting. In her present jellylike state, was Clarice in any condition to cope with him?

I groaned aloud and Samantha, in the corner of the kitchen by the Aga, interrupted her ablutions to stare at me through her huge blue eyes.

"It's all very well for you," I said glumly. "You can sit there by a nice, warm stove. I've got to go out in the rain. Aren't you glad you're a cat?"

Sam yawned; of course she was glad. No cat would even consider the infinitely inferior status of human.

So I emptied the buckets in the upstairs hall—they were filling faster today, I noted with a mental curse for my landlord—and headed for the Pettifers' new, watertight, sterile house.

I drove. The long walk in the rain last night had caused arthritic twinges in several joints I'd never noticed before, and I was also smarting from Alan's crack about driving lessons. I got insignificantly lost twice and, in desperation, drove the wrong way down a deserted one-way street to get to where I needed to be, but on the whole I thought I did rather well, though my knees were shaking as I got out of the car.

They shook even more on the front step as I considered the awful possibility that Archie might be home, but I was in luck. The door opened promptly to my ring and there, sturdy and blessedly sane and normal, was Mrs. Finch.

" 'Ere, now, 'ere's a treat for you, luv," she called in to the hall. " 'Ere's Mrs. Martin come to see you."

She stage-whispered at me behind her hand. "Wobbly on 'er pins still, she is, but comin' along. Company'll do 'er no end o' good."

"I'm glad you're still here, Mrs. Finch," I whispered back as I followed her into the kitchen, marveling a little. Here was a woman who had found a body, ministering calmly to the vapors of one who had only heard about it. Truly the Cockney is a rare and precious breed.

Clarice was looking better. What color she ever had was back in her cheeks and her soft, fair hair was neatly combed, if a bit discouraged-looking. She was sitting at the breakfast table in a becoming pink-flowered housecoat, with a teacup in front of her.

"Oh, Dorothy, I'm so glad to see you." Her voice was almost back to normal, too. "Won't you have some tea? Ada makes the most lovely tea, and frightfully good biscuits."

She sounded like a little girl inviting me to a dolls' tea party. I sat, and Mrs. Finch happily assumed her role of nanny, seizing the tea tray and making for the stove.

"I can't imagine what you must be thinking of me, Dorothy," Clarice went on shyly. "So silly of me to go to pieces like that."

"Don't worry about it. You had a shock."

"But I do wish I were more like you. You never turn a hair at frightful things, and nor does Ada."

I thought of Mrs. Finch's hysterics, but I didn't want to mention the murder scene. "It's easier for me. I'm still an outlander here, so terrible things aren't so—immediate, I guess. Besides, I've gotten good at hiding my feelings. Don't forget,

I've got more than twenty years on you. Anyway, I'm glad you're feeling more like yourself."

"You're very kind, Dorothy." There was a tear on her cheek; she brushed it away and pulled herself together. "But I mustn't be cosseted when I'm being foolish. I was afraid that Archie would be in trouble, you see, since it was the Town Hall. But the police have had the sense to realize he couldn't have had anything to do with it, so it's quite all right."

What a fragile bubble of hope! From what Alan had told me, neither Archie nor anyone else was out of the running at the moment. But let Clarice play with her pretty bubble while she could.

Mrs. Finch set a tray in front of us and waited, hands on hips, for applause. She certainly deserved it. The tray was beautifully arranged with a lace cloth, flowered china, and a mouthwatering plateful of scones and homemade cookies. I took a bite of one and rolled my eyes skyward, grateful not only for the goodies but for a reason not to reply to Clarice.

"This is sublime, Mrs. Finch. Do you ever give people your recipes?"

"We-ell. That almond biscuit's me granny's own receipt, and I said I'd never part with it but to me own flesh and blood. But seein' as 'ow me son ain't got 'imself a wife no more, nor yet no children—"

I caught my breath. "No children" was a phrase to be avoided around Clarice. One of our bonds was our childlessness, but whereas I'd learned over the years to deal with the pain, for Clarice it was fresh and new every single month, as her hopes were dashed again. I've seen her cry helplessly during a baptism at the cathedral.

This morning, thank goodness, her thoughts were otherwise occupied. "Ada's been telling me about the meeting last night," she said. "Do sit down and go on, Ada."

I breathed again. "Oh, were you there, Mrs. Finch? I didn't see you."

"I didn't like to leave 'ere, but me son went, an' come an'

told me about it after. I was just sayin' as 'ow it don't look too good for Mr. Pettifer bein' allowed to build 'is mall."

"Yes, but Ada," Clarice said eagerly, "last night was only a public discussion. Archie will talk them round, the Council and the people who matter. He's such a powerful speaker. And the important thing is that no one said a word about him being accused—involved in the—accident. I'm sure it was an accident, it must have been. Don't you think so, Dorothy?"

I was very glad I had a mouthful of biscuit, even if I nearly choked. "Certainly the police haven't made up their minds yet about the circumstances," I said after I'd taken as long as possible to chew and swallow. "At least according to the little I know. Could I have a little more tea? And Clarice, not to change the subject, but when do you think you might be able to get back to work? Mrs. Williamson really needs you."

It was rude, but it worked; Clarice is easily led. We talked about the bookshop for a few minutes, and then Clarice excused herself. "I'm having my hair done," she confided. "Ada thought it would brace me up."

"Good for you. Make sure they really pamper you."

I lingered in the hall after she had gone upstairs to dress. "What did your son really think of the meeting? I didn't want to talk about it in front of Clarice."

Mrs. Finch snickered. " 'Ee said it were a tea party compared to the one on Sunday."

"You mean the Lord Mayor's meeting?" I was all ears. "How does he know about that?"

" 'Ee didn't. I told 'im."

She looked at me, a cheeky grin on her weather-beaten face.

"All right, all right! How did you know, then? You know perfectly well I'm dying to hear all about it."

She sat down on the elegant Directoire chaise longue in the hall, an incongruous figure in a too tight nylon housedress, work boots, and white socks, and told me.

"See, the meetin', it was at the private room in the Feathers, seein' as 'ow the Mayor's Parlor is bein' done up. You know the Feathers?"

I nodded. It was the biggest pub in the High Street, a good place for food and drink.

"Well, Tom 'Arris, 'im as keeps the Feathers, is by way o' bein' a friend of mine." She looked up coyly, and I nodded and obliged with the wink that seemed to be expected. "So when we was 'avin' a friendly drop o' gin, like, 'ee told me all about it. There was just the six of 'em: 'is Worship, an' Mr. Pettifer, 'an Mrs. Dean as runs everything, an' then them as spoke at the big meetin'. That John Thorpe—" She sniffed disdainfully. "An' Mr. Farrell and Mavis Underwood, 'oo 'as got entirely above 'erself. An' the mayor thought 'ee could keep it all civilized, like." She affected a genteel accent. " 'See if we carn't all come to a meetin' of minds,' 'ee said. Wanted to see which way the cat would jump, if you arsk me, so's 'ee'd know which side to come down on 'imself.

"So for a bit it was all la-di-da and properlike. Then after dinner, when they'd all 'ad one or two, Mr. Pettifer started in. Talkin' big, like it was all settled, and lordin' it over Mr. Farrell.

"Well, Mr. Farrell, 'ee just blew up. The *language*, Tom said—such as you wouldn't 'ardly believe. A right down shindy, it were! An' Tom said Mr. Farrell just crashed out of there, like to took the door off the 'inges—an' 'ee said 'ee'd stop Archie if it was the last thing 'ee did, an' left lookin' fit to kill somebody!"

6

W HEN I G OT home, self and car amazingly still in one piece, I picked up the nearest cat and sat down on the couch to mull over Mrs. Finch's news.

Her sensational style made the most of the story, of course. When you got right down to it, all it amounted to was that the Lord Mayor's meeting had been less than cordial, and I'd already known that. Still, I now had the full personnel list and information about one specific run-in. What I didn't know was whether any of it was relevant.

I stretched to reach the end table (Emmy, who had purred herself almost to sleep on my lap, commented crossly) and got a pad and pen. Time to make some lists.

First I listed everyone who had been at the meeting Sunday night. Of course, there was no assurance that one of them was the murderer. But when six people get together and quarrel fiercely, and shortly thereafter a murder is committed that affects them all, in a site close to the meeting, my common sense refuses to dismiss the possibility of a connection. Very well:

Daniel Clarke, the Lord Mayor
Archibald Pettifer

Barbara Dean
John Thorpe
Mavis Underwood
William Farrell

Now, one of the first principles of criminal investigation, at least as practiced in my favorite form of fiction, is to establish who benefits. Or, as Hercule Poirot used to put it, to see what the real effect of the crime is and then determine who is better off because of it. And the most important result of this crime, to my mind, was that Pettifer's plans for the Town Hall were at least deferred, if not doomed. I studied my list of names. I'd lived in Sherebury long enough to know a little about most of them. Who was a likely murderer?

It was hard to imagine any personal benefit to the mayor. Aside from the sheer effrontery of suspecting such an important personage, I honestly didn't see that he had any ax to grind one way or the other. He had appeared, last night, to come down on the preservation side, but his motives seemed truly disinterested, with the welfare of the town foremost.

Pettifer was undoubtedly a loser at this point. True, he had access to the Town Hall, and he had acted peculiarly in the matter of tampering with the body. But I couldn't see any reason why he'd want to scuttle his own project.

Barbara Dean, I thought almost guiltily, looked like a front-runner. She had said that Pettifer had been in the ascendant Sunday night—and now she had the upper hand. Preservation was more than a preference with her, it was a religion. And she was a determined woman. To the point of ruthlessness? To the point of murder? I didn't know, but somehow I couldn't quite dismiss the idea. Her Eminence didn't let obstacles stand in her way, and she was used to getting what she wanted—somehow.

John Thorpe. Wealthy, the leading real-estate dealer in Sherebury, with a reputation as a sharp dealer, a hustler. I could imagine that ethics might play very little part in his actions, so he was attractive as a murder suspect. Unfortunately, he seemed to have no motive. He had shown last night that he was ready to throw Pettifer to the wolves if it was expedient. What a pity I couldn't figure out a private motive, so to speak. Could he have some grudge, a quarrel with Pettifer, so that he wanted to see him fail?

Mavis Underwood was an enigma. Unless she was a fine actress, she'd been genuinely furious about the prospect of the failure of the Town Hall Mall. But if her only interests were business-related, I couldn't see why another location wouldn't do just as well. And why would she want to cause trouble for Pettifer?

Which left me with William Farrell. I'd deliberately saved the best for last, and now I let myself take a good, long look. There was a lot against him. He wanted his own project to prevail. He'd quarreled, violently and publicly, with Pettifer the night of the murder. He was a powerful man with a hot temper. Yes, I liked Farrell a lot.

The problem was that I didn't have a single iota of evidence to support any of this theorizing. Until I had some answers about motive, and means, and opportunity—all the police-court questions—I was playing Blind Man's Buff.

I moved Emmy's tail off the pad and made another list of things I wanted badly to know.

QUESTIONS

Access to the scene of the crime: Who had a key to the Town Hall? Where are the keys now?
Who is the victim? [That was one for the police, though.]
Is there another motive besides ruining Pettifer's plans?

And there was another way to look at those ruined plans, I suddenly realized. If this murder—and it was murder, I was sure—were never solved, it would still stop Pettifer in his tracks. Suspicion is just as bad as proof for a politician, and Pettifer was nothing if not a politician. His position on the City Council was, in his mind, only a stepping-stone to greater things. If someone wanted to stop his political career badly enough to murder some unfortunate vagrant and plant the body . . .

Far-fetched? Perhaps. At any rate it was an unproductive train of thought at the moment. Until the body was identified, I reminded myself again, what I was doing was mere speculation.

And when had that ever stopped me?

Emmy grunted irritably in her sleep and moved her tail back where she wanted it, covering most of the page. I retrieved my pad, studied my meager notes, and sighed.

There certainly wasn't much inspiration there. As usual, list-making had made me feel busy while accomplishing exactly nothing. What I needed to do was talk to people.

Right, said the internal killjoy who gives me trouble every now and then. *You're going to go see a lot of people you don't know, any of whom might be a murderer, and ask them a lot of very snoopy questions. Have you lost your mind completely this time?*

I'll be subtle about it, I argued with myself.

Hmmph! You're about as subtle as a Mack truck.

Shut up. I'm American. They think talking to me doesn't count.

You can't get by with that one anymore. You've lived here a year, they know you're here to stay. If you don't get yourself killed first.

SHUT UP! This is only a game, anyway. Probably the kid fell downstairs or something and none of these highly respectable people had anything to do with it.

Then how did he get in the closet?

That, I answered triumphantly, is what I intend to find out by talking to people!

The killjoy shrugged its figurative shoulders, murmuring something about geriatric Nancy Drews, but I ignored it.

I concentrated on how to approach the people on my list. I knew two of them, of course, which didn't make it any easier. Barbara Dean would ignore any questions she didn't want to answer, and freeze me out in the process. And Pettifer—I just plain didn't want to talk to Pettifer. We'd been slightly acquainted for six months; it hadn't been a pleasure. Neither of us had found any reason to modify the mutual dislike that had crystallized at first sight. I didn't approve of his ambitions, and he thought me a reactionary, interfering busybody.

He had a point, in a way. Mind you, I'm not one of those people who are automatically against progress, but I have no time for the attitude that change and progress are necessarily the same thing. Something new is not guaranteed to be better than something old; it is, in fact, very often much worse.

Look at my house. (I stretched and did so, lovingly; Emmy protested.) After four centuries it needed work, true. Wood changes its shape through the years and adjustments must be made. But there was no problem with the structure itself. The craftsmen who put this house together knew what they were doing, and they took pride in their work. Joints were designed to bear the load they were given. Materials were chosen carefully for the job they had to do, especially the oak, so achingly difficult to work with but so strong and tough and durable—and so beautiful.

Perhaps that was at the heart of it. They cared about beauty then, those long-dead carpenters, and the glaziers who joyously let in the light. Those tiny diamond panes spoke not only of glassmaking techniques in the seventeenth century, but of the artisans' love of grace and proportion.

Whereas men like Pettifer—

Emmy, sensing my tension even in her sleep, sat up with a low growl and blinked at me, her claws pricking my leg.

"It's all right, cat. I won't hurt you. I don't think I'd hurt anybody, but it's sure a temptation with some people."

Better safe than sorry, Emmy decided, and leapt from my lap, landing with a heavy thud. That woke Samantha, who exploded from a featureless lump on the hearth into a lean bundle of energetic mischief. The two streaked into the kitchen, hissing and spitting. I climbed off my mental soapbox, put another log on the fire, and reconsidered my list.

Save Pettifer for last, anyway. How to tackle the others, then?

I hadn't the slightest idea how I was to arrange an informal conversation with the Lord Mayor, whom I had never met. Leave him for the moment. Of the others, the easiest was undoubtedly Mavis Underwood. If you keep a shop, you must expect people to come into it. I'd probably have to buy something, but information might be cheap at the price.

John Thorpe wasn't hard, either. I didn't look forward to a conversation with him, but he was an estate agent, and, like Mavis, had to expect the public to appear at his door from time to time. I even had an almost legitimate excuse: I was going to have to do something about my housing problem soon, either buy this house or continue to rent it, or find someplace else. Very well, call on him after Mavis.

Again I saved Farrell for last. He made me nervous. (The killjoy gave a little cackle at that thought.) Not, I insisted defiantly, because he was a murderer. Of course, I didn't really think that. He was just—scary.

And all right, so I'm not always perfectly logical, I told the killjoy as I struggled to my feet and prepared to go shopping. So sue me.

I chose one of my favorite hats, a crimson straw cloche decorated with a single huge poppy. It's extremely becoming, and the white silk dress piped in red that goes with it takes off at least ten pounds. I didn't care if my attire was more suitable for a Buckingham Palace garden party than a small-town shopping (and snooping) expedition. I knew I looked good, and I needed the self-confidence.

Besides, when you're overdressed, people tend to patronize you, and patronizing means underestimating. I could use that advantage, too.

I enjoyed the walk. The rain seemed to be over. It had made the paving stones slick and I had to watch my step, but it had also brought out heavenly smells as only a summer rain can. The freshness of growing things and the earthy aroma of wet stone and the elusive scent of water itself made me feel as if I were breathing in nourishment.

The sun came out just as I turned into the High Street, and a rainbow arched itself across the sky, so lovely that I stopped in my tracks and blocked the sidewalk. The beautiful jumble of buildings—Tudor, Jacobean, Queen Anne, Georgian—sparkled in the sun, their roofs and chimney stacks and small-paned windows all at irregular angles that caught the light and threw it back in generous sprays. Color sprang up out of grayness: the pink and red of small, handmade bricks, the subtle blues and greens and rusts of lichen-covered slate and tile roofs, the sharp black and white of half-timbering, all set off by the bright arc curving against retreating clouds. I don't know how long I would have stood there stock-still, tears in my eyes, but a small man ran into me, muttered a reproachful "Sorry," and then turned to look where I was looking. He grinned then, said, "Nice, innit?" and tipped his hat before hurrying off.

Underwood's occupies a central position on the High Street, across the street from the Town Hall and down a few doors. I'd been inside only once, trying to find something that would do for a niece's wedding. I hadn't found it.

The shop (the gaudy sign over the door spelled it "Shoppe") was deserted. Scarcely had the bell over the door stopped tinkling before Mavis bore down upon me, steely determination in her eye. Aha, the look said, a live one. I was grateful for the morale-stiffening hat.

"Mrs. Underwood?" I smiled brightly. "You won't remember me, I haven't lived here very long—"

"Mrs. Martin, isn't it?" Her smile showed even more teeth than mine. "How nice to see you again. Are you looking for a gift, or treating yourself?"

"Actually I'm just window-shopping," I said firmly.

Mavis was not to be deterred. "Well, then, let me show you something I know you'll love. They're just in, and they'd be lovely in your *exquisite* house. Brass occasional tables, genuine Indian work, and practical, as well—they nest, you see. Aren't they charming? Or perhaps you need something for your kitchen . . ."

I let her adamantly genteel tones wash over me, nodded and smiled until my face hurt, and waited for an opportunity to ask questions. It wasn't going to come soon. She didn't intend to let a customer escape her brightly varnished talons. I studied her inventory for something that might conceivably be of use, if only for a gift, and wouldn't cost an arm and a leg. The stuffed chintz cats and rabbits were attractive, but what would you do with them? Ashtrays—pretty, but nobody smokes anymore. Finally, desperately, I picked up the smallest china cottage I could find and interrupted her lavish praise of a wildly expensive brass bedstead.

"How much is this?"

Her face fell for only an instant. Never irritate a customer; she might buy something worthwhile next time. "You do have an eye for a bargain, Mrs. Martin! It's a lovely little cottage, isn't it, and only sixty pounds, including VAT."

I swallowed hard. The thing fitted nicely into the palm of my hand. "I am tempted," I lied gamely. How many plants for my garden would sixty pounds have bought? However— "I like it, you see, because it's so beautiful and old-fashioned. I just love your old English buildings! That *gorgeous* Town Hall, for instance. I understand it's going to be renovated, now that the offices have moved out?"

Her eyes narrowed a bit; I noticed the right eyelash was about to fall off. "Why, yes. As a matter of fact, my new shop is to be in the Town Hall Shopping Mall. Far larger and more convenient; you'll like it, I'm sure."

"Is that a fact!" My voice dripped innocent admiration, but her face was shrewdly speculative and I thought I'd better play it safe. "Actually, I did go to the meeting last night—maybe you saw me there—but I couldn't follow everything that was said. It's so hard for a foreigner, you know, the various accents and all. There seemed to be some opposition, though—or did I misunderstand?"

Was I laying it on too thick? No, apparently my hat was doing its trick. Mavis shrugged; the very short skirt of her bright green linen suit hiked yet higher, and her voice became confidential, her accent more like the one she'd been born with.

"There are always a few old bas—a few fuddy-duddies who want to stand in the way of progress. Just between you and me, if something isn't done, I'm closing this shop. I tell you, most days I could stand in here in me knickers and there'd be nobody to notice! Archie Pettifer has the right idea, but that man Farrell—not, I suppose, that it makes all that difference to me at the end of the day. If William Farrell wants to put up a mall at the edge of town where there's no foot traffic at all, I daresay the punters—uh, buyers, will come in cars, and my shop will fare just as well there."

"Oh, yes, Mr. Farrell. Frightening sort of man, I thought."

Mavis allowed herself a throaty chuckle entirely unlike the bright, tinkly laugh she had been affecting. "You ought to've seen him Sunday, if you were frightened last night."

"Oh?" Such a useful little word.

"The mayor had a few of us to dinner, you see, to talk out the project before the public meeting. Just those who were most involved." She preened a little, smoothing her hair with one beringed hand. "And Farrell was a trifle upset, as you might say. Those big hands of his—I thought he was going to strangle Archie, I really did. Of course he'd been drinking a bit, but I didn't know where to look, I really didn't. And he stormed out looking like murder."

I could, myself, have murdered the mother who came in at that moment with her noisy and obstreperous five-year-old. Mavis's attention was instantly transferred to the little boy, who represented a hazard to her stock approximately equal to a freight train, and I was forced to stand around fiddling with china dogs and tin boxes with pictures of Sherebury Cathedral on them. I was sure Mavis had more to say.

When the mother finally dragged her son away—without buying anything—Mavis turned back to me.

"Honestly!" she said. "The nerve of some people!"

I shook my head in hypocritical sympathy. "I was sure that child was going to break something. I guess some people have nothing better to do than take up a shopkeeper's time." I managed that line unblushingly, too. "You were saying about Mr. Farrell? This is *so* interesting," I added in a coo that would have startled my friends considerably. And where I dredged up the Atlanta accent I have no idea; I'm from Indiana.

But the moment had passed. "Oh, old Farrell has a hot temper. I reckon he cooled off soon enough. He really wouldn't harm a fly."

"It's an interesting coincidence, though, that someone actually did die that night, and in the Town Hall, too. I suppose Mr. Farrell has a key?"

I had no reason to suppose anything of the sort, but Mavis took the bait.

"Well, as a matter of fact, he does. I happen to know. It was his wife's. She worked there, you know, when I did, years ago. She's been gone now for over a year, but he kept the key. I know, because he told me so. Wondered who he should give it back to, now that the building's closed up."

"Oh, his wife—er—left him?"

Mavis stared at me. "You could say that. She died."

"Oh, dear. Did you know her well?"

She shrugged. "Not bl—not likely. I was just a typist, she was in the Planning Office. Of course, I was never meant to work in an office—too stifling. It wasn't until I got a job at a gift shop that I discovered my real mission in life. Not that it was as nice as this one." Her eyes swiveled, surveying her domain lovingly, possessively.

"You do have some lovely things. You must be very proud of your achievement."

"Yes." Her mind was firmly back to business. "Now, about that cottage. Or would you prefer this one? It's a bit more expensive, but it's Anne Hathaway's, you see."

I bought the smaller cottage in the interests of continued goodwill; maybe I knew someone who'd like it for Christmas. I was on my way out of the shop, the bell tinkling over my head, when I stopped and turned as if I'd had a sudden idea.

"Oh, by the way, I don't suppose you still have your key to the Town Hall? I dropped an earring when—well, the last time I was in there, and I don't like to bother the police about such a little thing."

The thick makeup couldn't conceal the hard lines that suddenly set in Mavis's face. "No. No, I don't. I turned it in when I left my job. I'd report that earring to the police if I was you, or they might think—I mean, you finding the body and all—"

She left the thought unfinished, but it was clear enough.

"Actually, Mrs. Finch found the body, but I see what you mean. Thank you so much—good afternoon."

Snooping was expensive, I thought indignantly, plodding down the street. Sixty pounds, and what did I have to show for it?

Well, I knew a little more about keys. Farrell had one and Mavis didn't. Or at least that was Mavis's version. Come to think of it, why had a mere typist had one in the first place? But if Farrell really did still have a key—he had a terrible temper—he left the meeting wanting to kill somebody.

That was the second time somebody had used that expression about Farrell. But the somebody he wanted to kill was Pettifer, and Pettifer was still alive.

No, at the price, my information was no bargain. Onward, Dorothy.

7

THORPE AND SMYTHE occupied an ugly, modern building on the High Street, next to the Tudor black-and-white that
housed a number of offices, including William Farrell's. In my
hurry to get past the ogre's den, I nearly missed the estate
agency; the only noticeable thing about it was the window display of house pictures with descriptions and breathtaking
prices. I opened the door, a bored clerk pointed me in the direction of Thorpe's office, and I knocked and went in.

John Thorpe was a stocky man who looked a lot like Michael
Caine, and talked like him, too, his nasal accent grating on the
ear. His suit, though impeccably cut and obviously expensive,
was just a shade too blue; so were his eyes. I tried not to wince
when he shook my hand with a bone-crushing grip. "Delighted
to meet you, Mrs. Martin. And how may I be of service to your
good self?"

"Well—" I launched into the almost true story about my waning
lease and the planning permission delays. "And I thought it would
be just as well to look at some other houses, because I really don't
know when the Planning Committee's going to get its mind off the
Town Hall long enough to consider my house."

If I hoped that would give me a lead-in to my real agenda, I was wrong. John Thorpe hadn't gotten to be a highly successful businessman by going off on tangents. "Quite right, madam. I can see you're as astute as you are charming!" A good many very white teeth flashed in a very sincere smile. "Now, I happen to have an especially fine property on my books at the moment, made for you, I assure you. Only two years old, in perfect condition, no need to worry about any repairs for years to come—and no fuss with the regulations when repairs do enter the picture!"

He showed me a picture of the ghastly place, all pebble-dashed concrete and shiny new brick, and followed with several others almost as awful. I finally stemmed the flow.

"These are all lovely, Mr. Thorpe, but I really prefer old houses. I know they're a lot of trouble, but—oh, what I really want is to stay where I am. After the meeting last night, do you have any idea when the Town Hall question might be settled?"

"Well, as to that, we all thought it was settled, didn't we, until—however. If you were at the meeting, you do understand I can take no sides, no sides at all. John Farrell has a good case, a very good case indeed."

"He seemed to be an angry sort of man. Someone told me he had a fight with Mr. Pettifer?"

Thorpe spread his hands deprecatingly. "Bit of a slanging match, that's all. Farrell has a temper, right enough, but no stomach for a good fight. Oh, there were words, words I couldn't repeat to a lady, I don't mind saying. But Farrell's got no stamina for the long pull, y'see. Got to be ready to get your teeth in and hold on, in this business." He laughed heartily at his mixed metaphors, his own excellent teeth showing to full advantage.

"Oh, my, it sounds—exhausting."

"No, no, just business. A lady like you wouldn't understand, of course. And no need!" He patted my shoulder.

I hoped he didn't hear my teeth gritting. When I could unclench my jaw, I opened it to ask more questions, but Thorpe suddenly realized we had strayed far from my ostensible purpose. "But enough of unpleasantness. Now, about your house—"

My supply of insincerities exhausted, I stood. "Unfortunately I have an appointment, Mr. Thorpe. I wish you'd keep me in mind, though, if a nice old house in good condition comes on the market." I gave him my address and telephone number, and turned to go. "Oh, there is one thing you might be able to do for me."

"Anything at all, of course." He expanded visibly.

Mavis Underwood had been suspicious, and Thorpe certainly knew just as well as she did when I'd last been in the Town Hall, but it was worth a try. "You see, what with the—unpleasantness—the other day, I managed to lose an earring in the Town Hall. I haven't liked to ask the police about it—such a little thing—anyway, would it be too much trouble for you to lend me your key so I could look for it? It's a pair I particularly like." I smiled winningly, my head to one side in a nauseating Shirley Temple imitation.

Which didn't work. Thorpe's smile froze into place.

"Ah, well now, what a pity. I regard that key as a solemn trust, Mrs. Martin. I never let it out of my possession. Never. Of course, I shall be more than happy to search for your earring the next time I am in the building. Though I should have thought the police would have found it. I'd report it if I were you." He shook my hand, and showed me out the door with more enthusiasm over my departure than he had displayed a few moments before.

Excellent advice, I thought as I walked slowly down the street, if my ridiculous story were true. Not that either Mavis or John Thorpe had believed a word of it. Oh, well. At least I'd confirmed that Thorpe had a key, too. Or said he still had it. And that he doubted Farrell had enough backbone to murder anyone. And he had, I was afraid, begun to develop some suspicions about me.

Did that matter? Perhaps not, unless he was the murderer. Then it might matter very much indeed. Alan would not be pleased if I got myself into a dangerous situation he then had to get me out of.

I shook my head impatiently. I could take care of myself. I'd just have to be a little more subtle from now on, that was all. At any rate Thorpe obviously thought me a "lady," and therefore negligible. Much as his attitude grated, it was useful under the circumstances. Dismissing him and Alan from my mind, I went on to the next thing.

It was time I met Mr. Farrell.

By this time I had walked to the end of the High Street. I stopped and stood for a few minutes staring sightlessly into a window displaying orthopedic appliances. There was plenty of afternoon left, and it had turned into a beautiful day. There wasn't the slightest reason why I shouldn't call on Farrell.

Except that I was scared.

And why? I demanded of myself. Just because he looks like every movie monster you've ever seen? Be your age.

I sighed rebelliously. Why does being one's age always involve doing things one doesn't want to do? Surely I'd earned the right to be irrationally scared if I wanted to. And why was I involving myself in something that was none of my business anyway? I could go have a lovely cup of tea and some sinful pastries somewhere and forget all about murders.

And call myself a coward for the rest of my life.

I turned around and walked back to the gorgeous black-and-white.

It was one of Sherebury's finest buildings, pure Elizabethan, with both beams and plaster carved wherever decoration could be applied. I'd wanted to see the inside of it for a long time.

WILLIAM FARRELL, BUILDER, was listed with a room number on a sign by the massive front door. I took a deep breath and pushed the door open with a dentist's-office feeling in my stomach.

The English don't use a standardized numbering system by floor, the way American buildings do, so room seven could be anywhere. As I stood in the dim hallway, delaying, I drank in the linenfold paneling, the heavily carved plaster rose on the ceiling with its accompanying crystal chandelier—much later period, that, but it fit—the gorgeous brass hardware on the heavy oak doors—

"May I help you, madam?"

I turned so suddenly I nearly lost my balance. He'd approached silently, on rubber-soled shoes, and stood towering over me, looking annoyed and bored.

Boris Karloff, in person.

I gulped and tried to get my breathing back in order. "No, thank you—well, actually—yes, I was looking for you."

"Yes?"

Never had the monosyllable been more intimidating. I took a deep breath, and some guardian angel supplied my barren brain with an idea. "Yes," I said firmly. "To talk to you about my house. Do you suppose we could go to your office? I'm getting a crick in my neck, looking up at you."

The atmosphere lightened a little. The jutting jaws moved slightly in what might have been meant for a smile as he gestured wordlessly toward the door to the right.

He seated me in the visitor's chair, sat down himself, and raised formidable eyebrows. I took a moment to study him and collect myself.

I hadn't been mistaken about the Frankenstein's monster face: cheekbones sharp enough to cut yourself on, with great hollows underneath, incredible shoulders, great awkward red hands dangling from too short coat sleeves. A man of about forty, he wasn't ugly, really, just craggy and very, very determined-looking.

He cleared his throat, but I didn't let him remind me what a busy man he was.

"Mr. Farrell, what was this building originally?" I wanted to get him talking.

To my great surprise, when he relaxed his face fell into lines more reminiscent of Gregory Peck—still craggy, but without the menace. "It was built to be a wool merchant's house, in 1562. His name was Thomas Lynley, and he was probably the wealthiest man in Sherebury at the time. There are records that the house cost one thousand pounds, which was an enormous sum then; the average workman earned about six shillings a week, if he was lucky."

He leaned forward as he spoke, his huge, ugly hands waving with enthusiasm.

"Was that the Lynley who endowed the hospital?"

"His son. You know some local history, then? You are Mrs. Martin, aren't you—the American lady?"

"Oh, dear, I'm always forgetting to introduce myself. Yes, I'm Dorothy Martin, and no, I don't know much Sherebury history, really, but Lynley's Hospital is one of the sights. You certainly have it all down pat; are you a Sherebury native?"

"No, I've settled here only in the past year, but there's been the odd job in the area now and again, and architectural history interests me. A hospital back then, you know, was an almshouse, a place of shelter, for the old or needy rather than the sick. Lynley's Hospital was endowed to provide a place for twenty old, indigent men to live out their days in comfort and decency. Their clothing was provided, as well as food and a daily ration of ale, and even a tiny income, enough to give them some self-respect."

"And it's still functioning, isn't it?"

"Not only functioning, but thriving—and on the original endowment, at that! That money has grown to a trust so formidable that additional charities have had to be added in order to try to fulfill the donor's original intent. A corresponding institution for old women was built in the eighteenth century, and early in the nineteen hundreds the whole lot were modernized, electricity and plumbing and so on."

"Oh, dear! They haven't spoiled it, I hope?"

"My dear madam," he said impatiently, "if ancient buildings are to be used, they must be made to meet modern needs—if it can be done. This building, admittedly lovely, is badly suited for offices."

"I admit I was surprised to see you in this setting. From what you said at the meeting the other night, I'd have thought you'd prefer something starkly modern."

"I should, if something suitable were available." He looked at his watch and frowned. "Now, Mrs. Martin, what can I do for you?"

"I shouldn't have come without an appointment, I know, and I've been wasting your time. But I was hoping you might be able to help me with my house." I gave him a brief version of my housing woes. "I know historic work isn't your specialty, but I'd hoped you might make an exception."

Boris Karloff returned, forcefully. "Even though you've hired Herbert Benson to do your roof. And you thought I despised old buildings."

I should have known—the Sherebury grapevine at work again. "I haven't hired him!" I said, stung. "He hasn't even looked at it yet. And I—I've tried everyone who—"

"Mrs. Martin, why are you here?" His voice could have etched glass, and it scared the truth out of me.

"I wanted to meet you."

The eyebrows looked incredulous. I floundered on.

"I was next door, talking to Mr. Thorpe, and thought I'd see if you were in. I'm snooping, if you really want to know. It's about the Town Hall, you see."

His jaw muscles tightened, and so did my nerves. I swallowed hard. "You can throw me out if you want to. You'd have a perfect right. But I think I have a right to ask questions, too.

Not only did I find the body, but I'm worried about Clarice Pettifer. She's a friend, and she's extremely upset over the Town Hall murder. Do you think her husband had anything to do with it?"

He looked down at his desk for a very long moment, those big hands clenched. When he finally spoke, his voice was quiet enough, but taut. "I'm not the right person to ask about Archibald Pettifer, Mrs. Martin. If you've been speaking to Thorpe, you know I've no time for Pettifer, nor he for me. I'd be sorry to learn he was a murderer, but not entirely surprised. And now, if you'll excuse me, I am late for a meeting."

He stood and opened the door, and if his tone was just short of rude, I could hardly blame him.

I made one last, feeble try.

"I don't suppose you'd have time to let me in the Town Hall on your way? I've lost an earring, and—"

"No." The monosyllable was unequivocal, and uninformative. He nodded curtly as he showed me out the door and shut it firmly behind me.

And I'd learned nothing about a key, nothing about a motive. All the same, it hadn't been a total waste of time.

Those hands of his, those frightening hands, didn't quite match. The right one was bruised and swollen and scratched, all across the knuckles.

THE MINUTE I got home, I put in a call to Alan.

"I'm sorry, Mrs. Martin," said his pleasant-voiced secretary. "Mr. Nesbitt is in London today, and I don't expect him back until quite late. May I give him a message?"

"No, that's all right. Or—you might just ask him to call me when he gets a chance. Nothing important."

I felt as if my lollipop had been snatched away. Here I was with all sorts of lovely new ideas and no one to tell.

As I mulled over my information, though, it seemed to lose a lot of its vitality. Pettifer and Farrell had quarreled bitterly on the night of the death. Everyone at the Lord Mayor's meeting apparently possessed a key to the Town Hall, or had at one time (though Barbara Dean was still an unknown quantity). And Farrell's right hand was a bloody mess.

I grinned as I imagined Alan's response to that still (in England) very improper adjective. It was true enough, though, and my best piece of news—if the police didn't already know about it. Did I dare call Inspector Morrison and ask? Probably not. My unofficial position was too precarious. No, until Alan got back there was really nothing to do but mind my own business.

You could call on the Lord Mayor. Or how about your friend Mr. Pettifer? Since you're so determined to play girl detective.

If I must keep telling myself what to do, I thought bitterly, I do wish I could manage to keep from being so blasted sarcastic about it.

WHEN I WOKE up Thursday morning, I lay wondering why I felt pleased, and then remembered. My roof! Mr. Benson was coming to fix my roof! And maybe we could start on plans for the rest of the alterations.

"Well, girls," I said to the cats after I finished breakfast, "we may actually know, soon, whether we're going to keep on living here. You don't want to move, do you?"

They lay blinking at me sleepily, each in her own patch of the sunshine that streamed in the windows. Summer was once more acting like summer, the sky a gorgeous blue with decorative little puffy clouds. Samantha was stretched out full-length on the window seat whose blue cushion went so well with her blue eyes. Esmeralda's green ones were mere slits that closed again as she snuggled luxuriously into the corner of the couch.

No, they didn't want to move. Cats are territorial animals. And so am I.

I couldn't settle to anything with Mr. Benson coming. He hadn't said when he'd be there, and it was a perfect day for gardening, but the minute I got good and muddy, he'd turn up. I'd spent the preceding afternoon in a self-righteous fit of house-cleaning, so the house was spic and span, and I'd promised myself no more sleuthing until I could consult Alan. So I fidgeted around, annoyed the cats, picked up a couple of books and put them down, and wrote two entirely unnecessary letters, growing more and more impatient.

Part of my agitation was due to a change in barometric pressure, I realized as I looked out the front window for the twentieth time. England's weather can change between breaths; those puffy little clouds I'd admired earlier were beginning to mass and build, and the temperature was dropping. A thunderstorm was coming before the day was out, and there would go a little more of my roof.

Mr. Benson and the rain arrived at almost the same moment, in midafternoon. A large, cheerful-looking man with a ruddy face that spoke of long hours in pubs, he was at the moment somewhat bedraggled. The rain was the cold, mean-spirited sort that veered with the wind from moment to moment, now flinging itself at the parlor windows, now beating against the front door and soaking the poor man thoroughly. As I let him in, a thunderclap followed a lightning flash so quickly that we both jumped, and Sam and Emmy streaked up the stairs.

"What the—?"

"Oh, sorry, just my cats. They're terrified of thunder. I'm *very* grateful to you for coming out in this weather, but goodness, you're wet! Would you like a towel?"

He peeled off his raincoat and dropped his umbrella into the stand. "No, no, not to worry. Not sweet enough to melt, am I, now?" A massive hand squeezed mine; I tried not to wince from the pressure of his rings. "Herbert Benson, at your service." He smiled genially, patting his bright brown hair. Nature never made it that color, I thought with amusement. He was probably afraid the dye would rub off.

"Come and have some tea, then. The roof can wait a few more minutes, and I've laid a fire in the parlor."

The storm increased in fury as we sat over cinnamon toast and tea (Mr. Benson's laced with a little bourbon to keep out the cold). He had excellent opportunity to observe the drafts eddying through my house. As the fire leapt and danced to the caprices of the wind, he waved a bit of toast toward the curtains rippling gaily at the closed windows.

"You could do with new windows, couldn't you?"

"I certainly could. Much as I love those tiny old diamond panes, they don't keep the weather out anymore. But new ones would have to look just like the old ones. This is a listed building, you see."

He rolled his eyes skyward. "Oh, yes, endless regulations, and a positive prejudice against nice, weathertight, plastic windows. Can't be helped, but it's a pity, all the same. However. Shall we see if there's anything left of that roof of yours, eh?"

I led him to the upstairs hall, where generous new leaks had appeared. We spent a few minutes racing between kitchen and landing with most of my collection of pots and pans, the extent of my problem having made itself dramatically apparent.

When we'd taken care of the immediate emergency, Mr. Benson asked me to show him the attic access, and disappeared. I listened apprehensively to bumps and thumps for a good half hour before he climbed down, as dirty as a chimney sweep and almost as wet as if he'd been outside.

Once he'd cleaned up a bit and settled back in the parlor, Mr. Benson shook his head mournfully.

"Bad news, I'm afraid. You need a new roof, from the timbers out. Oh, ta, don't mind if I do—no, no, that's quite enough.

There's no point in repairing it, the whole lot is going to go soon. Now, I can put down a tarpaulin for you as soon as the rain stops, and order in the tiles—"

"Slates," I said. "You may not have had the chance to look when you came in—the rain started just then. But it's a slate roof. And of course—"

"—it must remain slate to please the nosy-parker authorities," he finished, and sighed. "Cost you a packet, that will, take longer, too. Blasted nuisance, these regulations. But I'll keep a sharp eye on costs for you, Mrs. Martin. You may trust me for that." He rose.

"Actually, it's my landlord who'll be paying for it, but I'm sure he'll appreciate your care. How soon do you think you could get me an estimate?"

"Now, don't you worry about a thing, my dear," he said expansively. "I'll have it for you just as soon as the rain stops and I can get my men up top to measure. We'll do you a good job. And then we can take a look at those windows."

"Yes, and the other things I want done as well. Mr. Benson, you've taken a load off my mind."

We shook hands on it (carefully, on my part), and I spent the evening happily planning the details of my kitchen.

ALAN CALLED JUST as I was ready for bed.

"Sorry, did I wake you? I've been in town all day, but I've only just got back to the office and found your message, and I'm off again tomorrow for the next few days."

"No, I'm glad you called, though it wasn't all that important." The rain pattered against the windows cozily, and plinked into various pots and buckets, not so cozily. "I do have some news, though. I've found someone to work on my roof! And maybe draw up plans for the rest of the work as well."

"That *is* good news, indeed!" His weary voice relaxed into warmth. "What shall we do to celebrate?"

"Come for dinner," I said promptly. "We can roam all over the house and gloat about how nice it's going to be. When will you be back?"

"Late Sunday. Would Monday be convenient for you?"

"Fine. Sevenish—or whenever you can make it."

"I'll put you on the schedule for seven on the dot as an unbreakable obligation," he said firmly. "Rank ought to carry *some* privileges."

I fell into a peaceful sleep despite the ragged percussion section still operating in the upstairs hall.

The next couple of days, however, were disappointing. On Friday I awoke to brilliant sunshine and went off to the bookshop confidently expecting to see a tarp on my roof when I got home. All morning I glanced out the window whenever I got a chance, which wasn't often. Clarice still wasn't back, and this time Mrs. Williamson hadn't been able to find a replacement, so I was left to cope alone with the crowds of tourists brought out by the beautiful weather.

There was still no tarp when I got home, so I called Benson and got his answering machine. It was nearly six when he called back, sounding harried.

"*So* sorry, Mrs. Martin. Three of my men didn't turn up for work today, and I was hard put to finish a job we had in hand. They're an unreliable lot, some of these local lads. But the weather is expected to hold fine now for a few days, and we'll be out straightaway on Monday morning. And I promise you, if it rains, I'll lay your tarpaulin myself!"

I had to be satisfied with that, and it was true that the weather stayed beautiful—which actually added to my troubles, since my weeds reacted to sun and warmth by growing several inches a day. The cats, for whatever reason, had a two-day attack of the crazies, that unexplainable burst of hyperactivity known and feared by cat owners everywhere. And to top it all off, Jane, who would have commiserated with me, was down with a summer cold.

So I made chicken soup, left it (by gruff command) on her back doorstep, and fretted alone. By Sunday I was more than ready for the calming influence of the Church.

Sherebury Cathedral is a marvel of late-medieval architecture, designed in the fifteenth century for but one purpose: to lift the spirit to God. Five hundred years later it still works its miracles. Even my worst moods can't stand up to the soaring arches of carved stone, the brilliant stained glass, the quiet but intense drama of the Eucharist, and some of the finest liturgical music in England. At the end of the service, feeling exalted, I joined the line for coffee and buns in the parish hall, still humming the last hymn under my breath.

"You sound cheerful, Dorothy." Margaret Allenby, the dean's wife, stood at my elbow.

"I am—now. It hasn't been a very good week, but the service this morning was a great restorative."

"I'll tell Kenneth, he'll be pleased. Are you really feeling yourself again, after such a frightful shock?"

Jungle drums again. "Oh, I'm fine. The one who worries me is Clarice Pettifer. I saw they were both in church this morning, but she looked like death—did you notice? White and shaking, and her eyes all red. She hasn't been to work at the bookshop since it happened, you know. I wonder if the dean should have someone call on her?"

"Call on whom?" The dean came up to us, beaming, a tray in his hands. "I saw you two languishing back there and fetched us all some sustenance. Shall we try to find a place to sit?"

The parish hall has been adapted from the old scriptorium, the lone survivor, besides the church itself and the chapter house, of the medieval monastery that flourished on the site until the days of Henry VIII. The building, filled with the light the monks needed for their exacting work of copying and illuminating sacred texts, is otherwise ill-adapted to the needs of a large and busy twentieth-century parish, being full of stone pillars that obstruct traffic and interfere with furniture arrangement. We squeezed with difficulty into a corner, negotiating treacherous folding chairs, and the dean warily set the tray of coffee and buns down on the tippy table.

"Call on whom, Mrs. Martin?" he asked again, raising his voice. All those pillars and the stone surfaces of walls and arched roof create echoes that make normal speech impossible.

"Clarice Pettifer." I repeated my story. "I'm very concerned about her, but I hesitate to go over there again. If I happened to run into Mr. Pettifer, it'd probably make things worse—we hiss and spit at each other. Figuratively speaking," I added hastily, and the dean found it necessary to cough into his handkerchief.

"Anyway, Mrs. Finch—do you know Mrs. Finch?"

"Since we were children," said Margaret, who was Sherebury born and bred. "She's chapel, all her family always were, but her mother was one of the cathedral cleaners and used to bring little Ada along. I was a bit older, and we used to play together. Now she's taken over the family stand, comes in one day a week to do the brass. She does a lovely job, but I do try not to get talking with her, at least if I'm in a hurry—"

"Because you'd be listening till Christmas," I said, laughing with her. "I know. Anyway, she's been looking after Clarice from time to time, but I think Clarice needs to talk to someone who'll let her get a word in edgewise. Something's bothering her, and I can't figure out what."

"I'm glad you told me," said the dean. "I can't do it myself, I've no time. Sometimes I wish I'd never taken on an administrative post; it leaves me so little energy for any real pastoral work. But I'll speak to Canon Richards; he knows her quite well, I believe. The Pettifers are not at all regular churchgoers, of course, but she's a very loyal volunteer."

"I know. I think Mr. Pettifer comes mostly to be seen and do a little politicking, and brings her along for window dressing. It didn't work very well this morning, I shouldn't think. They were barely speaking to each other, from the way it looked."

Someone was trying to get the dean's attention, waving and inching toward us, smiling as he excused his way through the crowd.

"Mr. Dean—" I gestured and he turned, trying without success to push his chair back.

"Ah, Lord Mayor! I'm sorry, I don't seem able to stand up at the moment. However—do you know Mrs. Martin?"

"Daniel Clarke," he said in reply, shaking my hand. "Delighted to meet you, Mrs. Martin."

I'd never seen the Lord Mayor up close before. Without the trappings of his office, it was somehow even more obvious that he was a man to be reckoned with. I noticed the very keen eye, the alert tilt to the head—oh, yes, this man had earned his office.

"I'm so sorry, Kenneth, I know this isn't the time or place, but with the festival less than a week off there are a few details I do need to check, and I'll be away for a few days, so if you don't mind—"

"Yes, of course," said the dean. "We'll have to go elsewhere, if we're to hear ourselves think. If you'll excuse us, ladies—oh, I'm so sorry, Mr. Wellington, I didn't mean to back right into you—"

The dean finally pushed himself out of the tight corner and led the Lord Mayor away, while Margaret and I finished our coffee.

"They're two of a kind, those two," she said with a fondly exasperated sigh. "Kenneth should leave the details of the music festival to the canons responsible, but he can never feel that anything is really properly done unless he's seen to it himself. And Daniel Clarke is exactly like him. Small wonder neither of them ever finds time for a holiday."

"He's a conscientious mayor, then?"

"Oh, yes, I should think so. Of course Kenneth and I try to stay away from town politics, but one can't help hearing things."

Indeed. I suppressed a grin.

"And people do say he's hardworking, and incorruptible. Which of course makes him unpopular in some quarters."

"I didn't think there was such a thing anymore as an incorruptible politician."

"We-ell, Daniel isn't exactly a politician. At least, he is in a sense, of course. He's been on the City Council for a donkey's age, and they finally elected him head—which gives him the title Lord Mayor, you know. But his primary interest, I think, really is the welfare of the town, rather than his own ambitions. His people have lived here for generations, time out of mind— he's actually connected with the Lynleys, through his great-great-grandmother, or something like that. You know the Lynleys?"

"Not personally," I said with an attempt at a straight face. "They've all been dead for a hundred years or so, haven't they? But of course I know who they were, more or less. Richest people in town, endowed everything in sight, and so on."

"There's more to it than that, actually." As people were beginning to go home, the noise level was dropping so that Margaret and I could talk in some comfort. "In a sense, the Lynleys and their extended family built Sherebury. They put up a lot of the money for the abbey—the first abbey, the one that burned down in the fifteenth century, you know, and then again the present one."

I nodded. The cathedral in use today had been begun in 1415 to replace the eleventh-century Cistercian abbey, destroyed by fire in 1402. With blinding speed, in abbey-building terms, the church was completed in 1504. One short transept leading from the choir to the cloisters had survived the fire, and the monks had been just about ready to tear it down and rebuild it to match the rest, when the dissolution of the abbeys intervened. For over a hundred years the abbey buildings had languished, houses had been built on the grounds (mine among them), and decay had set in, until the political climate changed and the old abbey was repaired and designated a cathedral.

Margaret was still talking about the Lynleys. "Several of them were abbots over the centuries, and later, deans, when it was made a cathedral. One was even a bishop, not a very effective one, early in Victoria's reign, I think that was. And, of course, the family laid out the street plan as the city began to outgrow its walls. I could go on, but the point is the Lynleys have been a power in Sherebury for—oh, nearly a thousand years, I suppose. Daniel actually lives in Lynley Hall, though he had to buy it; it had been out of the family for a generation or two. So one can see why he has a protective interest in the town."

"Indeed," I said thoughtfully. One could also see why he might be distressed about Pettifer's plans for the Town Hall. A man who liked to take matters into his own hands—I wished I'd noticed his hands while he stood next to me. I was going to have to find an excuse, somehow, to get better acquainted with the Lord Mayor.

ALAN'S DRIVER DELIVERED him right on time Monday evening.

"Good, you're being driven, that means you can have a drink or two. When's he coming back to take you home?"

"I'm not going home," he said with a grimace that turned to a laugh when he saw my face. "No, I don't mean what you think I mean. I have to go back to the office to clear a huge stack of paperwork. So I can't drink much, or I'll fall asleep at my desk."

"Well, we'll start with something good, then," I murmured, very busy pouring Jack Daniel's into brandy snifters. I was glad I could excuse myself to the kitchen for a little last-minute soufflé preparation; it gave me time to recover from the ridiculous blush.

Alan and I had agreed, without ever saying a word, that we were not of the generation that fall into bed before knowing each other's full name. The circles we move in actually tend to the old-fashioned practice of waiting until marriage vows have been exchanged. Still, there was enough serious attraction between us that we'd given the matter some thought. At least I had, which was the reason for the blush. But, unsure as I was about the nature of our relationship, I wasn't anything like ready for it to take that kind of turn, so I was profoundly glad, when I got back to the parlor, that Alan had forgotten the subject.

"Do you want to tell me about your house first, or shall I make my report?" he asked, settling himself in my squashiest chair with Emmy on his lap.

"Report?"

"On the Town Hall body."

"Oh, yes, please!"

He smiled. "You sound exactly like a well-brought-up child about to be given a present."

"It's the way I feel. You're not always so forthcoming about crime, when I'm involved. I'm thrilled!"

"I'm not sure I've anything very thrilling to tell you, but for a start, we've identified the body. HOLMES tracked him down for us."

I giggled, as I always do when the acronym for the police computer system is mentioned. Who would ever suspect the British police of a sense of humor? Emmy looked up, offended until she decided I wasn't laughing at her.

"And what did Sherlock discover?"

"Not a lot more than a name, actually. The man's fingerprints were easy to identify, because he had a minor criminal record—joyriding, assault, petty larceny, that sort of thing. His name is Jack Jenkins, he was twenty-three years old, and he lived in Sheffield."

"Sheffield! That's a long way away. What was he doing in a little backwater like Sherebury?"

"That, of course, is one of the things Morrison is eager to discover." He scratched under the cat's chin and her purr filled the room with organ music. "There's the obvious connection, of course."

I shook my head. "I may be dense, but . . ."

"Pettifer. He's from Sheffield, you know."

"No, I didn't. I didn't even know he wasn't a Sherebury native. But Alan, that sounds serious!"

"Not really. It may mean nothing at all. Sheffield is a very large city indeed. Just because two people were born there doesn't mean they know one another. The crew are working on Jenkins's connections in Sheffield, but his associates don't like talking to the police, and apparently he had very little family. Just his mother, so far as anyone has said, and she seems to be out of town. Something may turn up there, in time. The curious thing, though, is that Pettifer isn't the only one in the case with a Sheffield background."

"You're going to make me ask, aren't you?"

He lifted his glass and drained it. "I'm not being coy, really. It's only that it seems like *lèse-majesté* even to mention the name of Barbara Dean in connection with a suspected murder."

I choked on my bourbon. When I had finished snorting and could speak again, I shook my head and croaked, "Oh, Alan! Surely not. I admit I'd thought of her, but only because she was at that meeting and is opposed to Pettifer. Really, I'd almost as soon believe the Queen had something to do with all this. You don't actually think—"

"I don't think anything at this stage, and neither does Morrison. He's gathering information, that's all. Do you want to hear the results of the autopsy?"

I thought of my lovely dinner, nearly ready in the kitchen. "How gory is it?"

"Not bad at all."

"Come in the kitchen and tell me, then, while I put together a salad. I'm sorry I can't offer you another drink," I added, pointing at his glass. "We've drunk it all—I keep forgetting to stock up."

"Just as well. Now, I've already told you," he said, gathering up Sam, who was trying to trip him, "about the head injury. That was the cause of death, as Morrison thought. The medical examiner found another one, just a bad bump, really, that he thinks happened some little time before death, so there may have been a quarrel that went on for a bit. Quite a wide range for time of death, because so many variables are unknown—they say from nine P.M. to two A.M. And then there's the bruise on the chin. Some scratches there, so the ME has guessed the murderer may have worn knuckle-dusters. It would explain why the blow was so effective; it actually broke the jaw, though it was the crashing of the head into whatever it hit that did the job. I gather you don't want all the medical details."

"Not really," I agreed. "I notice you've stopped qualifying yourself every time you say 'murder,' though."

"The injuries couldn't have been self-inflicted, and no one delivers a punch like that to the jaw by accident. The inquest hasn't been held yet, and all sorts of routine inquiries are still grinding along—tracing Jenkins's movements, and everyone else's, that sort of thing—but murder does seem the only reasonable possibility at this point."

"Then all we have to do is figure out what a petty crook from Sheffield was doing in the Town Hall, and why someone wanted to murder him," I said, taking the smoked salmon from the fridge. "Here, guard it with your life. That and a spinach soufflé are most of dinner—catch her!"

Sam managed to make off with only a little of the salmon, and my house is solid enough that the chase didn't damage the soufflé much. We put the cats out and sat down to our meal in peace.

"You haven't told me anything about your house yet," said Alan. "I didn't notice any signs of roofing."

"There aren't any. And my enthusiasm has dimmed considerably. The man I asked to do something about my roof isn't keeping his promises."

Alan raised his eyebrows. "Who is he?"

"His name is Herbert Benson."

The eyebrows rose still further. "Pettifer's friend?"

I smacked my hand on the table. "That's it! I knew I'd heard the name somewhere. He's the one Pettifer was drinking with, the night of the murder—the alibi. Good grief, and I thought I could trust him!"

Alan chuckled. "Having a pint or two with Pettifer surely isn't enough to make a man untrustworthy."

"Maybe not, but add his failure to show up when he said he would—twice, now—"

"Did he give you a reason?"

"The first time he said he was shorthanded—some of his men didn't show up for work," I admitted grudgingly. "Today I couldn't reach him."

"Unreliable workmen can happen to anyone. Give the man a chance. But if he doesn't work out, what about Pettifer himself?"

I put my fork down. "Alan, are you out of your mind? He'd never stoop to such a plebeian task as a new roof. And I wouldn't let him even if he wanted to. The man who's going to desecrate the Town Hall, working on *my house*? The man who's driving his wife into a nervous breakdown? And probably a murderer, to boot?"

"You do love jumping to conclusions, don't you?" said Alan calmly. "Have some more of this excellent wine of yours and listen for a moment. First, Pettifer has done nothing to the Town Hall thus far, and he won't unless and until planning permission is given. Second, I don't know what the matter with Mrs. Pettifer is, and neither do you. It may have nothing to do with her husband. Third, a man is innocent until proven guilty in this country. I believe you've heard of the system."

I glared at him. He appeared not to notice.

"Finally, whatever else he may be, Archibald Pettifer is an excellent builder, and I doubt his men have a great deal of work just now. Dorothy, I don't like the man myself. He's arrogant and pretentious and a social climber and all the rest of it, I freely admit. But he doesn't feel to me like a murderer, and I confess I have some sympathy for him just now. This Town Hall project is an abomination, of course, but it was the dream of his life and his chances of completing it grow dimmer every day that this murder is left unsolved. Morrison says he saw him in church yesterday, and the man is disintegrating before one's eyes. You must have noticed, yourself."

Well, no, I hadn't. I'd had eyes only for Clarice. I pushed some salmon around my plate and avoided Alan's eye. We sat in silence for a moment.

"Alan," I said finally, "you have a talent for making me feel ashamed of myself. I think I've been childish about a number of things."

"Dorothy, I—"

"No, let me finish. I've been running around poking my nose into things, even knowing you wouldn't like it much. And you've made me see I've been unfair to Pettifer. I'd like to start over on a better footing. If Benson doesn't show up tomorrow, I'll call Pettifer. And I promise—"

"No," said Alan, putting his big, warm hand over mine. "Stop punishing yourself. You're not childish, just curious and independent and impulsive and very, very human. Don't make me any promises. Or—no, on second thought, I'll accept one. Promise me you'll look after yourself. I do care a great deal about what happens to you, you know."

He leaned over and kissed me on the cheek, so gently and tenderly that there were tears in my eyes when I tried to smile at him.

"Now," he said, pushing back his chair. "What delectable sweet have you concocted to finish off this marvelous meal?"

It wasn't until the middle of the night that I swam up out of insidiously pleasant dreams and realized I'd never told him about Mr. Farrell's injured hand.

9

TUESDAY MORNING CLARICE finally turned up at work.

"I sure am glad to see *you*! How are you feeling?" She looked awful, a lot worse than when I'd seen her last. Her sweater and skirt hung limply on a body that seemed at least ten pounds thinner, though she could hardly have lost that much weight in a week. She was making a brave attempt to keep the flags flying, however. Her hair looked all right, and careful makeup tried to hide her pallor and the purple circles under her eyes. Looking at those eyes, I wondered for the first time if she were really physically ill, not just upset. "Are you sure you're well enough to be here?"

She tried to smile. "I'm fine, truly. Canon Richards came to see me yesterday, and made me see how foolish I was to give way to my nerves over such a little thing. He says I'll be better out of the house, keeping my mind occupied. I hope we're busy today."

"Speaking of busy, I have a job that needs doing," I said, a little nervously. Might as well get it over with. "I know your husband is an important contractor, of course, and probably doesn't take on small jobs, but—"

The change of subject was a great success. Clarice's face took on some animation. "Oh, I'm sure he'd be happy to help you! He's just waiting, you know, for a decision to be made about the new mall, and now that . . ." Her voice trailed off, and I hurried into the breach.

"Yes, well, it's my roof, you see. It's leaking badly. I'm embarrassed even to mention it, and I wouldn't dream of bothering him ordinarily, but the people who usually do this sort of thing all seem to be booked up, and unless I get it repaired or replaced soon I may have serious problems. I did talk to Mr. Benson, and I don't suppose he'll be very happy if I give the job to someone else, but he hasn't done anything about it, and Alan thought—"

Clarice's chin lifted. "Herbert Benson?"

"Yes. Oh, that's right, you must know him, he's a friend of Mr. Pettifer's."

"A business acquaintance." There was no mistaking the frost in her voice. "You'd be *much* better off having Archie do the work. Shall I speak to him this afternoon?"

"I wish you would. Have him call me—ring me up, I mean." What on earth was Clarice's problem with Herbert Benson? Clarice gave me no chance to pursue that thought.

"I'm sure he'd like to work on your house," she went on with some vigor. "It's a very interesting period, you know—architecturally, I mean. I shouldn't be at all surprised to find a hidden passage or a secret room—a priest's hole or something like that, you know. There's a book here—if I can find it—" She rummaged around in the architecture section of the shelves, and finally pulled out a little volume with a cry of triumph.

"Here it is! *The Architecture of Dissent*. It's all about the Reformation and the Civil War and times like that, and the way buildings were altered to help people escape persecution. Archie has a copy; he's always been fascinated with that sort of thing."

"I'm sure there's nothing like that in my house; it's too small," I objected, but I took the book. It *was* intriguing. The secret passages that sound so fairy tale–like to an American were indeed a way of life in England's history, and I've always been interested myself, but I was startled to hear of Pettifer's fascination. It began to look as though Alan might be right about the man.

I was a little unnerved by the way Alan kept working his way into my thoughts. I was too old, I told myself, to go around mooning like a teenager over a kiss—a brotherly one, at that. And if I gave in, I'd get nothing else done.

I managed to close the mental door, but the hinges were a lot stiffer than I'd expected.

Clarice and I were as busy as she'd hoped, and as the morning wore on, it seemed that the canon's advice had been good. She went about her duties with a lighter step and her voice grew stronger and more assured. The crowd of teenagers that arrived just before noon, though, did her in. A school group from Birmingham, doing a tour of cathedrals just before their holidays began, they were noisy and demanding.

"You look ready to drop," I said as we were leaving for lunch. "What did those miserable kids do to you?"

"Nothing, really. They were only—being kids." Her voice was back to virtually inaudible.

"Well, I think you did too much. You'd better go straight home to bed. Or can I buy you some lunch first?"

"No, I'll have something at home, but thank you very much all the same. And I shan't forget to tell Archie to ring you."

There was that stubbornness again. Well, one couldn't hold the woman's hand forever, after all. She had to learn sometime to deal with life's vicissitudes. She hadn't even seen the body, for heaven's sake. There was no real reason why she shouldn't pull herself together. And if she was so eager to get home to Archie, let her. No accounting for taste, I thought with great originality as I waved good-bye and headed for home.

Pettifer phoned me before I'd finished my sandwich lunch. I was profusely apologetic about bothering him with such a small matter, and he was at least civil—a major step forward in our relationship. Furthermore, he was at my house an hour later, with two men to measure the roof, and when he sent them away and the two of us sat down to talk about the project, I began to think humble pie was going to be my dessert du jour.

"We'll have to tear off the whole lot and start fresh; repair any structural damage first, though from what I can see there's very little so far," Pettifer said authoritatively. "Now, what you want is slates that match the originals, and they're not going to come cheap if we have to buy them new. The best thing would be old ones that have already weathered. I'll ask about, see if I can lay my hands on some. There's a redundant church being pulled down over Bradford way with a slate roof; I might—"

"Yes, but Mr. Pettifer," I interrupted, "will old slate keep out the rain?"

He looked at me pityingly. "So long as they're not broken. They're used because they're durable, you know. And we'll reuse any of yours that we can remove in one piece. That way we'll still have the lichens, and you'll want them—nice, soft, old look they give the place."

I could hardly believe this was the same man who was so pompous in public, the man who wanted to do unspeakable things to the Town Hall.

"It's very nice of you to deal with this for me. You do realize the roof will have to be identical in appearance to the old one?"

"Yes," he said, reverting to his old manner, "I am familiar with the requirements of a listed building."

Well, it *had* been a stupid question, hadn't it? I studied the pattern on the carpet. "I'm sorry, silly of me. Of course you are. When do you think . . . ?"

"The men will be back with a tarpaulin within an hour or two, so you'll not have to worry the next time it rains. I'll have a cost estimate by Thursday at the latest. You understand it depends on what we find when we get to the timbers, but I can give you a range. The men can proceed as soon as you wish. Now, if there's nothing else—"

I stood. "Mr. Pettifer, you can't imagine how grateful I am to deal with someone who obviously knows what he's doing. My only problem now is to tell Mr. Benson I've given the job to someone else, and I'm not looking forward to it."

"My wife mentioned that. I shall be seeing him later this afternoon; I'll tell him if you like."

There was a look in his eye that told me he would be delighted to pass bad news along to his colleague, and again I wondered why, but lacked the nerve to ask.

"Yes, thank you again." I shook his hand. "Mr. Pettifer, I—we haven't always gotten along too well, and I—er—apologize if I was ever rude, or—"

"Not at all." With the all-purpose English nonresponse and a curt nod, he was out the door and I was left shaking my head and wondering if I would ever understand the man.

At any rate, he kept his promises. An enormous sheet of blue plastic arrived in short order and was firmly fastened down. Let it rain!

Not that it showed any signs of doing so. The English summer was still behaving the way the tourist brochures make you think it always does, with blue skies and enough heat to seem almost like real summer. Too much of the afternoon was left to fritter it away; my conscience drove me into the garden, trowel in hand.

An hour later, hot, dirty, and thoroughly fed up, I was knocking on Jane's back door.

"Is your cold better?" I asked when she appeared. "I sure hope so, for my sake as well as yours."

"Nearly gone," she said. "Soup did the trick. *Down,* sir!" (This to the friendliest of the bulldogs, Winston, who was eagerly raising his head to be patted.) "Beer?" she added, noting the sweat pouring down my face.

She produced it, cold and ambrosial, along with a couple of damp paper towels that removed the worst of the grime.

"I've had it," I announced after a life-giving swig or two. "That garden is defeating me and enjoying it. The only things that are thriving are the weeds. It needs someone to tell it who's boss. Do you know of a good gardener looking for work?"

"Thought you'd never ask. Bob Finch," she said promptly.

"Finch? Is he—?"

Jane nodded. "Her son. Likes his drink now and again, but works hard in between. Knows his business."

"Well, if he's anything at all like his mother, he's the man for me. He lives with her?" I downed several more cold swallows.

"Does now. Wife left him a few years ago; he moved back in with mum. Seems to suit both of them. He's company for her and she chivvies him back to work when he's on the drink."

I finished my beer and pushed my chair back. "Jane, you've come to my rescue so many times I'll never be able to repay you. There is no one else's kitchen in the world that I'd dare invade looking like this and asking a favor. And that's a dubious honor if there ever was one. I'd give you a hug if I were fit to touch anybody." Embarrassed, she muttered something and turned away to scold a dog, and I made off home to call Bob Finch.

Fortune was smiling on me today; maybe it had something to do with the sunshine. Bob was at home and sober, and would be 'appy to come over and 'ave a look at my problem.

He turned up a few minutes later in an amazing vehicle that had once been a pickup truck. A short, compact, wiry man of indeterminate age, he wore earth-brown garments that looked older than he did and gave him a distinct resemblance to a gnome. The watery blue eyes and ruddy nose trumpeted his alcohol problem, but his hands, today, were steady and as strong

as pieces of oak, and his weather-beaten face was honest, the
rosy-apple cheeks good-humored.

"Dear, oh dear, madam, let the place go somethin' shockin',
'aven't you?" He clucked accusingly and picked up a handful
of dirt, letting it sift through his fingers. "Good soil, that, too—
you could make a picture o' this 'ere place. Delphiniums along
the wall, see, with 'olly'ocks in the corners to 'old it all up, like.
Not too many roses, they'd be too fancy, except for some of the
old-fashioned ramblers on this 'ere fence. Daffs in the spring, o'
course, and snowdrops, and you want some lavender for the smell,
and then wallflowers in summer. Some cuttin' flowers, you'll want,
snapdragons and mebbe some asters and chrysanths . . ."

As he went on, gesturing broadly, it all materialized before
my eyes. Gone were the weeds; in their place a perfect English
cottage garden nodded drowsily in the soft breeze, birds sang,
butterflies skipped from blossom to blossom . . . I blinked, and
there were only weeds, with a little brown gnome standing in the
middle of them, pointing.

"That there mint, you got to dig it all out. Take the place,
mint will; put it in a pot if you 'ave to 'ave it."

"How long will it take?" I asked abruptly.

Bob blinked. "To get that mint out? I'd say—"

"To do it all. What you said—hollyhocks and snapdragons—all that."

"Given a free 'and, madam?"

"Absolutely."

"Four, five years." He saw the look on my face and went on
reassuringly. "Gardens takes time to grow proper. But I can 'ave
it lookin' tidy in a month or two, and get a start with bedding
plants, then we can add on, like."

"When can you start?"

The brown face split in a grin. The gnome spat on his hands
and rubbed them together. "I'll get me spade and barrow."

Three hours later my garden was transformed. Oh, it looked

awful, but progress was being made. Great piles of dirt and weeds punctuated an expanse of mud that overflowed onto the grass, with only a few isolated plants surviving; I was well satisfied.

"I'll be 'ere first thing tomorrer," he said as he climbed into his battered truck. "Cheerio!"

As I waved good-bye to my gnome I suddenly remembered we hadn't even discussed wages. Oh, well. Live dangerously. Whatever he charged, he was worth it.

THE NEXT MORNING the doorbell roused me at what felt like dawn.

" 'Ullo, madam, I 'ope as I 'aven't got you out of bed," said Bob, studiously ignoring my slippered feet and robed figure. " 'Ere's a list o' the flahs I thought we might put in, fer a start, like. Fer you to approve."

It was a matter of form, of course. Bob was going to plant whatever he wanted, with my heartfelt blessing. But I took the list, gravely thanked him, and got started on my own day while he went whistling about his work.

I had a good deal to do, but while I was trying to organize tasks Samantha jumped into my lap. Of course, once a cat has honored you with her presence, you can't insult her by getting up. I reached for reading material, and my hand lit on the book I had brought home from the bookshop the day before: *The Architecture of Dissent.*

I was absorbed in two minutes. The book was full of references to passages and priest's holes and secret meeting rooms, many of them in famous buildings I'd visited. Most, of course, were in the great country houses or public buildings, where thick walls could easily accommodate a passageway, and elaborate paneling was convenient to hide an entrance. Some of the priest's holes, especially, were made from perfectly ordinary back stairs or cupboards that had fallen into disuse, a concealed door being all that was required to convert them for devious use.

Great Scott!

My sudden movement startled Sam awake; she jumped down in alarm, but I scarcely noticed. I'd had an IDEA.

What if there were some hidden place in the Town Hall?

It would explain such a lot. Maybe the dead man had discovered something he shouldn't, and that's why he was killed. And his body was moved because it was too close to the secret whatever. And if there was some kind of treasure hidden in the place, it would explain why Archie was so anxious to get hold of the Town Hall at whatever price!

Some people never grow up. Blissfully refusing to let common sense intervene, I sprang up, grabbed the first hat I laid hands on in the dark hall closet, and took the shortcut through the cathedral to the Town Hall.

I was so full of my wonderful idea when I set out that it never occurred to me to wonder how I was to get into the place—nor what I would do if I found Mr. Pettifer in sole occupation. If I'd stopped to think at all I suppose I'd have assumed the police seal was still on the doors. But Providence is said to look after fools. When I came to a breathless halt at the massive front doors, they stood wide open and I could see Mrs. Finch toiling her way up the stairs with a mop.

"Yoo-hoo! Mrs. Finch! May I come in?"

She turned and beamed at me. "Mornin', dearie. You're a sight for sore eyes—specially in that 'at."

"What's the matter with my hat? I just—oh, dear."

I pulled it off my head, looked back at Mrs. Finch, and succumbed to a fit of the giggles.

The hat I had clapped on my head without a glance revealed itself in all its glory as the patriotic tricorn I had decorated for the Fourth of July, complete with white ribbon and one rakish red ostrich feather.

"Well, that'll teach me to look in the mirror before I go out, anyway. Come to think of it, though," I said in growing indignation, "Bob saw me when I left. He waved. Why on earth didn't he say something?"

" 'Ee's nearsighted, dearie, an' 'ee never wears 'is glasses when 'ee's workin'. Men 'as no eye for a 'at, anyway."

"He certainly has an eye for flowers, though. Yesterday he showed me a few things I had no idea were there—just puny little plants I would have pulled up as weeds. I'm so glad he's agreed to do my garden for me."

"Hmmph!" Mrs. Finch snorted. Not for worlds would she have admitted she was proud of her son's talents. "Mind you keep 'im up to the mark, now. 'Ee takes a drop now and again, there's no denyin', but not when 'ee's workin' proper. 'Ee'll do a good job for you, but you 'as to keep 'im to it."

There was an awkward little pause. Now that I was there, I felt a little shy about introducing my subject. In the face of Mrs. Finch's solid common sense, secret passages seemed awfully far-fetched.

"So you're back to work," I finally said inanely.

She snorted again. "Come to give the place a good dustin' an' airin' out one more time. 'Ee's told me I needn't come back." Her sniff left no doubt about who " 'ee" was. "Until they makes up their minds what's to be done with the place, I've lost me job 'ere. Not but what it was only the two days a week, an' there's plenty as want me to work in their 'ouses, but it's a comedown, and no mistake."

"Oh, I *am* sorry, Mrs. Finch. You're right, it's a slap in the face, after all you've done here over the years. But I'm glad you're here today, anyway, because—well—"

She looked at me inquiringly and I took the plunge.

"Well, it's probably silly of me, but I wondered if you'd ever heard any talk of any secret rooms or passages in the Town Hall, or—or anything like that," I ended lamely.

To my great relief she took me seriously and scratched her head in thought.

"Not in the Town 'All," she said finally, a thoughtful frown on her face. "There's the underground passages, under the streets, o' course—medieval, those are, for drains and the like. An' Lynley 'All 'as a priest's 'ole or two, an' there's 'oo knows wot all over the cathedral—but I never 'eard tell of anything 'ere. Barrin' the room in the attic, that is to say."

I scarcely dared breathe. "There's a secret room in the attic?"

"Don't know 'ow secret it is. It 'as a sort of 'idden door, but everybody knows about it. Everybody as knows the building, anyway. I can show you, if you likes."

It was better than nothing. My balloon was deflating rapidly, but I trooped up the stairs behind Mrs. Finch, the two of us wheezing and puffing in a geriatric chorus.

10

"MIND WHERE YOU step, dearie," said Mrs. Finch. "There ain't no real floor up 'ere, just them boards laid across the beams. One slip and you'd go straight through."

We were in the biggest of the attics, the central one with the gable windows. There was quite enough light on that sun-drenched day to show me the perils of my footing. The light showed, too, just how serious the Town Hall's condition was. Huge oak roof timbers were riddled with beetle damage; the dust we kicked up as we picked our cautious way across the floor was more than half sawdust left behind by the busy de-stroyers. Cobwebs hung everywhere in great, dirty festoons, and the smell of dry rot was overpowering.

"Mind your 'ead!"

The warning came too late. Watching the floor, I'd ignored what was above me, and fetched up against a hammer beam—this one still sound and extremely solid. I yelped and put up one hand to steady myself, the other, cautiously, to examine the damage to my temple—and then stood staring, openmouthed.

In the wall facing me, a door was slowly creaking open.

"It's that there beam," said Mrs. Finch stolidly. "You pushes on it to make the door open. Most people," she added, "uses their 'ands."

"I'll remember that next time," I said just as dryly. "It's a good thing I was wearing this silly thing, or I'd be laid out on the floor." I picked up the thick felt hat, brushed it off ineffectually, and, balancing on the unsteady floorboards, walked into the secret room.

It was a vast disappointment. There was nothing much there, just a small room with one dusty gable window and no door except the one by which we'd entered.

"Do they know what it was used for?" I asked my guide. I doubted it had been a priest's hole or anything so romantic.

"Papers," she said briefly. "Important dockyments, as they didn't want to get lost. They cleared 'em out an' took 'em to that new buildin' when they moved, though wot they wants with papers 'undreds of years old, as is crumblin' to bits besides, is more than wot I can tell you."

I took one more look around. Shelves lined the walls, empty except for thick dust and, in one corner, a forgotten piece of paper. I picked it up gingerly and shook off some of the fuzz; it seemed, so far as I could make out the faded, spidery handwriting, to be a tax roll of some kind for 1737, of interest possibly to historians but not to me.

Well, of such disappointments are the lives of superannuated girl detectives made. There was nothing in this room except decay. I tucked the paper into my purse to give to somebody who might want it and went back into the main attic, carefully avoiding the hammer beam. Mrs. Finch manipulated the beam to close the door, and we plodded back down the stairs in silence.

Perhaps, I thought dismally, the Pettifers of this world were right and this building needed a new purpose, a new life before it moldered to ruin. Signs of decay were all about me, now that I actually looked. Water-damaged plaster ceilings were stained and moldy; in places they had fallen. Paneling was beginning to crack and warp; floorboards were coming up; window frames were rotting. Only on the main floor had Mrs. Finch's efforts kept the wood shining and smooth, the ceilings and staircase intact.

"Well, thank you, Mrs. Finch," I said as we reached the front hall. "I thought we might find something important, but I suppose it was silly of me."

"Do call me Ada, luv," she said comfortably. "And don't you fret about nothin'. It'll all come out in the wash, you'll see. Wot was you goin' to do with that there paper?" she added. "On account of, it didn't ought to be taken away, like."

"Oh. I'd forgotten about it. Take it to the Civic Centre, I suppose, where the rest of them are. Although I do hate to drive out there."

"Or the museum, mebbe," Mrs. Finch—Ada—proposed. "It's just round the corner, and they'd know what to do with it."

"Good idea. Thanks again."

I stood in the brilliant sunshine of the High Street, my dusty hat dangling from my hand. I couldn't put it back on; the bump on my head was swelling fast. Besides, it looked ridiculous, and while I usually don't mind looking ridiculous, today I wasn't in the mood.

I was, in fact, both depressed and cross. I had been so sure I'd had a brilliant idea, and not only had it been exposed for the silliness it was, but I'd finally realized the desperate state of the Town Hall. I would have enjoyed having a temper tantrum on the spot, out of sheer frustration, but the influence of civilization was too strong.

Oh, well, I might as well take the stupid paper to the stupid museum and have done with it. Then I could go home and kick the cat, or something equally unfair and unproductive.

I stumped crossly down the street.

Sherebury Museum, tucked away in a dark little building

on a narrow side street, was a drab-looking place with a drab little curator, and very few exhibits of any real interest. The bell over the door tinkled as I entered.

"Good afternoon, madam. May I help you find something in particular, or would you just like to look about?"

His tone made it clear that he found either eventuality unlikely. He was a Mr. Chips type with the enthusiasm left out, a gray little man of about eighty in tired tweeds, who had obviously decided there was nothing in the museum worth looking at—or maintaining.

Oh, well, presumably he would know what to do with a stray piece of Sherebury history, and frankly, I didn't care much. I pulled the piece of paper out of my purse, trying not to tear off any more of the fragile edges.

"I happened to find this in the Town Hall just now. It's old and I thought the museum should have it. I don't suppose it's important, but anyway, here it is."

Mr. Chips took the paper from me, frowning in bewilderment over the tops of his granny glasses, as the doorbell behind us tinkled. A red-letter day, indeed—two visitors at once.

"Good morning, Mr. Pym."

The deep voice startled me, and I turned to see a large, looming form.

"Mrs. Martin." He nodded slightly.

"Good morning, Mr. Farrell," I said, and turned back to Mr. Chips—or Pym, I supposed.

"As I said, the paper may be of no importance, but it certainly doesn't belong to me, and I thought someone should have it who knows what to do with it. Do you suppose you could give me a receipt or whatever, just so there won't be any question?"

Mr. Pym looked at Mr. Farrell helplessly. "The lady found this, she says—I can't make out what it is or what she wants me to do with it."

Farrell shot a sharp glance at me. "Let me see."

The gray little man complied.

"Hmm. Part of an electoral roll, it seems. Where's the rest of it?"

The question was addressed to me. I shrugged.

"Search me. I found this in the Town Hall. I—er—went to see Mrs. Finch and she was—showing me some of the damage up in the attics. This was on a dusty shelf; there was nothing with it."

"I see. And did you find your earring?"

"What earring?"

The question was out before I had time to think, and Farrell's sarcastic smile was ample punishment for my witlessness.

"The one you lost the other day. Or had you forgotten?"

"I found it. Under my bed. So kind of you to ask." I smiled, showing as many teeth as possible, and gathered myself to return the attack. "I must say I'm surprised to find you here, Mr. Farrell. Given your modernist views, I wouldn't have thought history was your cup of tea."

Perhaps someday I'll learn not to let my mouth run away with me. Too late, I remembered that Farrell had displayed considerable knowledge and interest in Sherebury history.

"History is a fine thing in its place, Mrs. Martin. Its place is here, in museums, not trying to ruin lives in the twentieth century. And if you've been snooping about the Town Hall, I should think you'd have seen for yourself that such a ruin is no place for a shopping mall."

I was so upset at finding myself in agreement with him that I lost my head completely. "My snooping, as you call it, has to do with trying to find out who committed murder, not with civic disputes. I suppose you'd rather the question remained unresolved?" My tone was as nasty as I could make it, and little Mr. Pym shrank back nervously.

"As a matter of fact, I should!" Farrell shouted, pounding his fist on the counter. "So far as I'm concerned, doubt about that murder is perfectly splendid. Uncertainty is just as good as guilt any day for putting spokes in Archie Pettifer's wheels. I would suggest, Mrs. Martin, that you consider minding your own business from now on. An excellent policy, especially for foreigners! Good day, Mr. Pym."

He slammed my miserable electoral roll down on the counter, breaking off a corner in the process, and banged the door so hard behind him that one bell shook loose, fell to the floor, and rolled into the corner, tinkling madly all the way.

I W E N T H O M E with an ache in my head and determination in my soul, and picked up the phone.

"Alan, I need to talk to you. Would you be free for a few minutes if I drove out there?" Central police headquarters for the county are located in a sprawling complex just outside Sherebury, accessible by a busy highway and a terrifying double roundabout. I must have let some apprehension show, because Alan's voice developed a hint of a chuckle.

"Longing for a drive in the country, are you? I've an appointment at the cathedral at three to pin down security arrangements for the concert for our royal guest." The sigh was only a small one. "Supposing I call for you when I've finished with that, and we'll go to tea somewhere."

"Fine." It wasn't, actually. I wanted privacy to express my suspicions, and I wanted to talk *now*. But I could have tea ready for him, and preparing it would give me time to sort out my thoughts.

So I made sandwiches and cut them into crustless triangles, and whipped up a batch of cookies, and tidied away some of the cat hair that settles on every surface of my house. Alan was ringing my doorbell as I put away the vacuum cleaner.

"I see your roof work is under way," he said as he came in. "Benson or Pettifer?"

"Pettifer, much as I hate to admit it. At least he's covered it—we'll see whether he comes through with the rest."

Alan sniffed and changed the subject. "Is that peanut butter cookies I smell?"

"That's right, they're your favorite, aren't they?" I said brightly—as if I didn't know! "I thought we'd have tea here, if you don't mind. The cookies aren't proper tea fare, I know, too American, but the sandwiches are all right. How did your session go at the cathedral?"

Alan followed me into the kitchen and munched on a cookie as I heated water and arranged the tray.

"All serene there, I think," he said between bites. "We've all been through this so many times before, it was just a matter of going over the drill once more, with a few added touches to try to meet whatever additional threat there may be. Frustrating not to know what that might be, but—" he waved his hand in the air and scattered crumbs "—one does one's best. The dean is being perfectly cooperative, of course, as usual."

"That's nice." Alan looked up sharply, and I pulled myself together. "I'm sorry, I was thinking of something else. Alan, I may be making mountains out of molehills. I've had time to think about it since I called you, and I think I probably am. But I'll feel better if you tell me that. Shall we take this into the parlor?"

Prevailing English usage for the principal room of the house is "lounge." I think it sounds like a hotel or a bar and refuse to use it. On the other hand, "living room" is far too American for a house as old and English as mine. I've compromised on "parlor," and my friends accept it amiably as another American eccentricity. We settled down on either side of the fireplace, unlit on this warm and beautiful day, and I poured out the tea before I drew a deep breath and launched into it.

"You won't think I'm silly?"

Alan just looked at me. I've learned to recognize that look.

It means something like *Don't you know me well enough by now to know I take you seriously?*

"All right, then. Alan, I think William Farrell may have killed that boy."

He took a sandwich and bit into it thoughtfully. "Why do you think so? Any evidence, or just a feeling?"

"When you're as old as I am, feelings about people are perfectly legitimate evidence in themselves," I retorted. "They're always based on experience. But I know what you mean—police-court evidence. And I do have some. Has anyone working on the case noticed Farrell's right hand?"

He relaxed and took another sandwich. "Ah, his hand. So you saw that, too—and drew the perfectly logical conclusion. Yes, Morrison interviewed him personally, and got an explanation.

"It seems that our Farrell has quite a temper. He says that after the Lord Mayor's famous dinner party the night of the murder, he was extremely upset. He went home fuming about Pettifer and his plans, and by the time he got home, he'd worked himself up to the point of slamming his fist into the wall."

"He could be lying."

"Of course. But our people checked; the wall next to the door had marks of blood and skin on it, at about the right height. And the ME, who took a look at Farrell's hand, doesn't think the injuries could have been caused by contact with Jenkins's jaw. He's quite sure a bare fist couldn't have done so much damage to the jaw, either, not unless the fist belonged to a trained boxer—which Farrell certainly is not."

I was both relieved and disappointed. "Well. Then it looks as though he's out of it. But—Alan, his temper *is* awful! Two people, on separate occasions, told me he left that dinner meeting looking as if he wanted to kill someone—those were their very words. And this morning when I saw him, he certainly looked ready to kill me!"

"And when was that?" Alan's tone was mild, but his eyes narrowed and he put down a cookie.

"Oh, a perfectly innocent encounter in the Sherebury Museum. I went in to take—um, that is, I found something old, and . . ."

I floundered to a stop and Alan picked up the cookie again, and simply waited.

"Oh, all right, if you must know. Did you rise to your exalted rank by exploiting the power of silence in an interview?"

He said nothing to that, either. I rolled my eyes heavenward. "You are the most exasperating man! I had no intention of telling you I was poking around the Town Hall looking for secret passages."

"Ah. So that's it. And I presume you found the room in the attic?"

It was so deflating to have everyone at least one step ahead of me.

"Mrs. Finch showed it to me. I thought—oh, I suppose you might as well have all of it. I was off on a Nancy Drew tangent again. I thought maybe there was something hidden close to where Jenkins was actually killed. And maybe the murderer moved him to keep whatever it was secret. And if Pettifer knew about it—well, anyway, it seemed to hang together when it first occurred to me. But Mrs. Finch—Ada, I mean, I keep forgetting—she says the attic room is the only one in the Town Hall. And she ought to know."

"Have a sandwich; you're not eating anything," said Alan kindly. "It's a perfectly plausible theory, actually. We—that is, Morrison—thought of it, too."

"You did? I wasn't being totally ridiculous? I even thought he might have gotten his head injury on one of those beams—they're pretty low."

"Dorothy, you really must stop underestimating yourself, you know. The idea is sound, and we've investigated it thoroughly. Unfortunately, it looks as though Ada Finch is right. The plans for the Town Hall—the original plans, and drawings of alterations down through the years—have been kept. It's a remarkable piece of cultural history, actually, all in the Sherebury Museum. But when our people studied them they found no sign of anything except the attic strong room, and that's shown quite clearly. Of course, an addition that was really meant to be a secret would have been kept out of documents, so the men went over the building itself with a fine-tooth comb, measuring the depth of walls and so forth. They came up with absolutely nothing. So I'm afraid we know no more than we did about why the man was moved."

"Or by whom," I said, and sighed. "So that's that. As a detective I think I make a great—"

"Cook," Alan supplied, polishing off the last cookie on the plate. "So was it interesting, that 'something old' you found in the Town Hall?"

"No. Just a piece of old town records. I don't think Mr. Pym has the slightest idea of what to do with it, not that it matters. That museum is a disaster, Alan!"

"Another victim of a strained municipal budget. It needs more space and a proper curator, is all. The collection is actually quite good."

"Well, it doesn't look like it! Somebody needs to take it in hand."

He grinned at me as he heaved himself out of the overstuffed chair. "There's a project for you, my dear—just mind you keep out of the way of our bad-tempered Farrell. I must go. Splendid tea, Dorothy. By the way, what have you done to your hair?"

"Oh, just got tired of it and decided to experiment." I'd rearranged it to cover up the lump I had no intention of telling him about.

"Oh, I thought you might have bumped your head on one of those wicked beams." He grinned at my scowl, gathered me up in a brief but very efficient bear hug, and was gone; my musings for the rest of the day had nothing whatever to do with museums or murder.

11

B Y T H U R S D A Y M O R N I N G Bob was ready to start plant-
ing one small part of my garden, so I spent a few hours in the
delightful occupation of watching someone else work, now and
then offering a suggestion, praise, or even a little help. And early
in the afternoon Mr. Pettifer, true to his word, telephoned to say
that the plans and estimate for my roof were ready, and could
he drop them off straightaway?

He was there in ten minutes. I showed him into the parlor
and he got down to business at once. "Now," he said, "here's
the estimate. It's high, but not so bad as it might be because I
was able to pick up those old slates. And of course you'll get
some help from English Heritage, and/or the council."

He handed it to me. It took my breath away; I certainly
hoped a great deal of financial help would be forthcoming from
somewhere or my landlord was in danger of cardiac arrest.

"We'll match the original techniques and materials as
nearly as possible," he went on, "and the appearance will be
identical."

"I must confess I had a few qualms about that when I talked
to Mr. Benson. He didn't seem to realize that I *wanted* the house

kept the same; it wasn't just a question of complying with the authorities. By the way—uh—have you talked to him?"

"Yes. He wasn't best pleased, but he must learn to keep his promises. Nothing drives off trade faster than breaking appointments. I told him so." He smiled grimly.

"Yes, well—thank you for dealing with him. Now, once the financing is worked out, how long do you think the job will take?"

"No more than three weeks, given reasonable weather. There's nothing much on our plate at the moment." He grimaced and then shut his mouth firmly and looked the other way.

There was something about his unspoken comment that made me suddenly see him as a human being instead of a cardboard villain, and (as I often do and almost always live to regret) I said the first thing that came into my head. "Mr. Pettifer. You're obviously a good craftsman, with respect for fine old work. Why do you want to destroy the Town Hall?"

Mr. Pettifer gave me a look that would peel paint and stood, drawing himself up to his full five and a half feet. "Destroy it! I don't want to destroy it! I want to save it, make it of some use to the town! Where's the crime in taking a fine old building and using it for something different, putting people to work, getting new money flowing? I am fed to the teeth with all the do-gooders acting as if I was proposing to commit murder!"

I glared right back at him as anger stripped off what few restraints were left on my tongue. "Well, if that's the way you answer a civil question, I don't blame them! I asked because I wanted to hear your point of view, instead of just believing what everyone says. If you don't want to talk about it rationally, fine!"

"And what," he asked, purple in the face, "does everyone say?"

"That you used to be a fine builder before you fell in love with money and power. That all you care about now is your own advancement, no matter who or what stands in your way. That you've got enough influence to push through this Town Hall plan even though it's an absolute sacrilege, and the university housing project, too." I paused and then threw the last shred of caution to the winds. "That you bully your wife, and you probably killed the man in the Town Hall because he might have ruined your plans somehow."

There was a long pause. The house was very quiet. As I watched Pettifer's face, wondering if I should reach for the poker, I could hear the chink of Bob's tools in the garden, and even the lapping of Emmy's tongue as she drank some water out of her bowl in the kitchen.

"You speak your mind, don't you?" he said, finally, his color closer to normal. "I wonder you care to employ me if that's what you believe."

"I didn't say I believed it all. You asked what was being said. I told you."

"Yes. In reply, then, A: I am still an extremely good builder, with high standards. B: I do not find either the Town Hall Mall or the university housing project to be detrimental to Sherebury. My mall will save a magnificent building from destruction, and the Victorian houses I propose to replace with new flats are insanitary, ugly, and poorly built. I sincerely hope my influence is still sufficient to see that both proposals are approved. C: My relationship with my wife is no one's business but ours. D: I did not murder anyone. Good day, Mrs. Martin."

Whew! After he slammed the front door, I stood for a moment shaking my head just to make sure it was still on my shoulders. My record of winning friends and influencing people was growing more and more dismal. And all I'd done was ask a few honest questions. A few more and I wouldn't have a friend left in Sherebury.

It was just as well that I had an urgent errand to keep me from brooding about that nasty little encounter. Now that I actually had a cost estimate for my roof, I intended to ginger up my dilatory landlord by presenting him with the proper grant applications, all filled out and ready for his signature. I'd seen the forms, which weren't impossibly complicated; I could get them from the planning office this afternoon, complete them, and mail them to him tomorrow.

There were, I had learned, various legal recourses open to me if the landlord didn't act quickly. I was mulling them over, hoping very much I wouldn't have to use them, as I pulled into the Civic Centre parking lot and congratulated myself on still being alive after the drive.

I was in no way mentally ready for an encounter with John Thorpe, who was coming out the door as I went in.

He saw me, of course, and his eyes lit up. There was no escape; civility forced me to respond, if coolly, to his greeting and handshake.

"Ah, Mrs. Martin!" he boomed, bouncing on the balls of his feet. "I believe I may have some good news for you. We have a new house on our books—at least, an old house, ha, ha—that may be just what you're looking for. The moment I saw it, I thought of you. A Victorian rectory, marvelous old place, all sorts of charming woodwork and so on. In need of some tender, loving care, but I think it's just up your street. When may I show it to you?"

"Well—actually—I don't like Victorian architecture much, not the English variety anyway. And I think I've decided to go ahead and fix up my own house. I have the estimate for the roof here, as a matter of fact, just ready to submit with the grant applications. So you see . . ."

He saw, unfortunately, a good deal more than I intended him to. His geniality vanished. "Yes, indeed. Quick decision, wasn't it? Looking for a new house last week, staying in the old one this week? Just what *are* you planning to do, Mrs. Martin? Or don't you know?"

I stood my ground. I was tired of being bullied. Surely I

could do as I liked about my housing problem.

"I'm staying in my house. Definitely. I'm so sorry to have taken up your time before I made up my mind. If you'll excuse me—"

"Yes, well, there's no accounting for tastes, is there? I wouldn't stay in that house myself, the condition it's in. Who knows what might happen? But it's your funeral."

He nodded curtly and strode away. I picked up my forms and drove home, where I painstakingly filled in blanks for a couple of hours, posted the letter to the landlord whose existence I was beginning to question, and spent the evening with a nice, familiar Agatha Christie. I found it comforting to deal with something I knew the ending to.

I WOKE TO a fine drizzle on Friday morning. As I plodded across the Close to work, the murky light washed the color out of the world, and the cathedral seemed to brood, its great gray bulk hugging the earth.

Inside, though, the atmosphere was entirely different. The staff were arranging chairs and music stands at the east end of the nave, and marking rows of seats with numbers. Armies of volunteers scurried about with masses of flowers in their arms. Screeches and the voices of invisible technicians issued raucously from the sound system.

The cathedral was *en fête*. I had completely forgotten that the Sherebury Cathedral Music Festival began tonight. And I was going to the gala opening, a performance of Beethoven's Ninth Symphony by an extremely exalted orchestra.

With Alan.

My step was light as I walked into the bookshop.

Clarice evaded my inquiries about her health. "I'm fine," she said persistently. "Truly."

And not another word could I get out of her. Well, she looked more or less all right, if a bit droopy—but she was often droopy.

And we were too busy to talk, anyway. The hundreds of music lovers who had come to town for the festival all seemed to be whiling away the time in the cathedral. They raised a brisk trade in postcards and guidebooks.

At about eleven Barbara Dean blew in and came straight over to me.

"I've been hoping to speak to you," she said, "and this is the first moment I've had. Some of those volunteers!" She threw up her hands and rolled her eyes, and I remembered that she was (of course!) in charge of the front of the house arrangements for the music festival.

"If you're too busy, we can make it another time," I said hastily, but she was not to be deflected.

"No, no, I simply wished to know about your house. I see that you have a tarpaulin in place. I trust that means you have been successful in finding a contractor for the work?"

"Yes, thank you. The man recommended by Planning Aid, a new man in town named Herbert Benson, wasn't getting anything done, so I called in Mr. Pettifer, and he's given me an estimate for the work. I—er—I know you and he aren't exactly friends, but he does seem to be quite professional." She said nothing at all, and I hurried nervously on. "I mailed—posted the grant applications to my landlord yesterday."

"Good," she said briskly. "And you'll let me know if he doesn't respond?"

"Well—"

"Splendid. Good morning!"

The breeze as she swept out wafted three sheets of poetry off the counter.

When my shift was over and I'd had some lunch at home, I lay down for a nap. I wanted to be fresh and rested for the concert, and at my age, the way to be fresh in the evening is to sleep in the afternoon.

I had just settled myself comfortably, with a cat curled up

on each side and the rain beating a nice lullaby on the plastic-covered roof, when the phone rang.

"Afternoon, Mrs. Martin, Herbert Benson here."

"Oh, Mr. Benson, I—"

"Sorry about the little misunderstanding over your roof. No hard feelings, of course, but you might have let me know. *But* still, no use crying over spilt milk, eh? I have a quote for you on those windows we talked about. Shall I bring it over straight, away?"

"No! No, Mr. Benson, I don't want—"

"Ah, well, if this is a bad time I'll ring up again. Ta-ta!"

He had hung up before I could make some excuse. He reminded me of one of those hard rubber balls. The harder you throw it away, the faster it bounces back to you. Would I never be able to get rid of him? It was a good half hour before I could stop fretting and get to sleep. Even then, my dreams wrapped me in blue tarps and buried me under tiles and slates, and I woke with the sheets wound around me and the cats long fled.

It was an effort to work up any enthusiasm for getting dressed and going out, but I put lots of carnation bath oil in the tub and soaked for a long time in the bubbles, and when I'd applied careful makeup and gotten into my laciest, most feminine undies, I was myself again.

I hesitated for quite a while about the outer layer. I tend to overdress. If I'd been going by myself I wouldn't have cared, but I didn't want to embarrass Alan. I finally chose a slimming black silk sheath, topped off with a very chic scarlet jacket I'd bought for almost nothing in the Portobello Road. Pearls were always correct, and I put on and then regretfully took off a little black satin evening hat that I loved. I was cramming necessities into a small black beaded bag when the doorbell rang.

Alan didn't whistle; that wasn't his style. He didn't say anything, either. He just stood there in his immaculate black suit and regimental tie and looked me over with his careful policeman's eye, a smile slowly broadening on his mobile face.

When he spoke at last I could have kissed him. "Smashing. Absolutely top marks, except—where's your hat? You're not really you without a hat."

"I'll be the only woman in the place wearing one."

"What does that matter?"

"Alan, I do love you," I said gratefully, and flew upstairs to get it.

"It's stopped raining," he said as he held my raincoat for me, "but it may start again at any moment. And will you ruin your shoes if you walk on the wet path?"

"Yes," I said. "That's why I'm wearing wellies." I slipped out of my black patent heels and into a pair of yellow rubber boots, and we set off across the Close, arm in arm and well pleased with ourselves despite the glances that greeted my eccentric ensemble and the shoes dangling from one hand.

"How is your roof holding up in the rain?" asked Alan as we made our way up the nave looking for our seats.

"Fine, and Pettifer's come through with the plans and cost figures." We'd reached our row, second from the front, and had begun to excuse our way past the knees. "Now if my landlord will get a move on, and the grant applications can actually make it through the planning bureaucracy—oh, heavens! I'm *so* sorry!"

For in scrambling past a very large, pillowy woman I had slipped, and grabbed the first thing that came to hand to keep from falling.

It happened to be the head of the man in the front row.

And the man in the front row happened to be Daniel Clarke, Lord Mayor of Sherebury.

If I could have vaporized I gladly would have. Or better yet, been beamed up to the *Enterprise*, to return in a time warp a few seconds ago with the sense to be more careful.

Somehow one survives these things. I apologized profusely to everyone in sight, was established by Alan's firm hand on my elbow in the seat directly behind my victim, and hid behind my program until a shaking of my chair caught my attention. I peeked out to see who was moving it, and why, and saw that Alan had nearly reached the point of apoplexy with suppressed laughter.

I could have killed him, but when he caught my eye he snorted loudly and had to reach for his handkerchief to cover more unseemly demonstrations, and I began to giggle myself. It was perhaps fortunate for all concerned that the conductor came out just then and we had to behave. I wasn't sure I would make it through the politenesses at the beginning, with all the dignitaries welcoming everyone, but when the music began I forgot everything else.

Beethoven's Ninth Symphony isn't easy to program. It's too short to make up an evening by itself, really too long for a second half, and too spectacular for anything to follow it. Tonight's conductor had chosen the conventional route, beginning with a short Haydn symphony and giving us a long intermission to prepare for the master. It was at the intermission, just as I was feeling calm and comfortable, that the Lord Mayor turned to speak to me.

"It's Mrs. Martin, isn't it? I believe we were introduced last Sunday."

A politician needs a good memory for names and faces, but I would have been much happier to remain his anonymous assailant. However, I acknowledged my identity while Alan, infuriatingly, stood smiling and silent by my side.

The Lord Mayor went on. "Did I hear you say you're having some difficulty with grant applications, or something of the sort? Is it possible that I might be of some help? Mrs. Dean mentioned something to me a day or two ago."

I was awed. So La Dean could talk even the Lord Mayor into

dealing with a peon. I muttered something inarticulate and Alan, at last, came to my rescue.

"Mrs. Martin is eager to get the roof question settled quickly, since her lease will expire soon and there is a good deal of further work to be done on the house, as well." He explained about my conditional purchase offer.

"Oh, dear, dear. Well, I shall certainly do all I can. Your house is quite lovely, Mrs. Martin, and essential to the character, not only of your street, but of the Close, since it can be seen from the cathedral. We cannot allow our finest buildings to perish from neglect, can we?"

Here he was interrupted by the dean.

"I'm so sorry, I must go and attend to some details, but I shall speak to you again, Mrs. Martin. I shan't forget."

Well, no, he probably wouldn't forget the woman who had nearly snatched him bald.

"That color is very becoming," murmured Alan.

I hoped he was talking about my jacket, not my face, but my blush ebbed as I mulled over what the Lord Mayor had said. He was concerned enough about Sherebury's architectural heritage to go out of his way for a stranger.

Was he concerned enough to commit murder?

That one so distracted me that I surfaced again only when the baritone launched into his fourth-movement solo, and then I tried to dismiss everything but the music from my mind. But a niggling thought kept insisting that the brotherhood of man espoused by the "Ode to Joy" was a lovely idea, all right, but even the first pair of brothers didn't get along any too well.

In fact, one of them had killed the other.

12

DEARLY AS I love England, every now and then I reach a stage of acute frustration with its pace of life, and with the relentless politenesses and restraints. By Saturday, having gotten exactly nowhere with a solution to the murder, and chafing under the delay with my housing problem, I was more than ready to spend the weekend with American friends in London, celebrating the Fourth of July.

It did me good. The Andersons are two of my favorite people, and the party was marvelous. Tom is some sort of exalted vice president of a multinational with a lot of American employees in London, and every July 4 they throw a big shindig at the company headquarters, a country estate on the Thames. A picnic, brass bands, fireworks—the whole bit, including a tour of the mansion. I hadn't liked the idea of a big manor house being turned into offices, but after I saw how tastefully it had been done, I came back to Sherebury on Monday morning thoughtfully considering a new aspect of the preservation question. Surely it was better to put a glorious old house to a new use than to let it decay because no family could afford to live there anymore.

Much as I detested Pettifer's plan, it was sounding more and more logical.

The cats pointedly ignored me, as punishment for my absence. When I sat down at the dining-room table, however, and began to open my mail, the rustle of paper was too much for Samantha. She dived onto the table, claws extended.

"Ouch! *Bad* cat! You know you're not allowed up here—and you've been told before about those claws. Scat!"

I had to crumple an envelope for her to chase before I could get rid of her. Sucking on a scratched knuckle, I turned over the letter she'd attacked. It had survived pretty well, with just two neat punctures where she'd grabbed it between her teeth.

It was nothing very interesting, just a note from friends asking how I was and saying they missed me. Not important at all, except that the Davises live in Sheffield.

"Sam, it's a sign," I informed her. She stopped in mid-chase, all four legs stiff, brown tail quirked into a question mark. "I hadn't been sure whether I ought to pursue this thing anymore, but here's an excuse to go right to the heart of the mystery. Now, I certainly can't turn it down, can I?"

I waved the letter, which was a mistake. Sam leapt into the air, neatly seized it from my hand, and killed it.

After a hasty lunch, I poked my head out the back door to check the weather. It had been deteriorating all morning; the air hung still, hot, and heavy under a sullen sky.

"Is it going to rain, Bob?" He was hard at work on my back flower bed, seemingly impervious to the heat.

He sat back on his heels and studied the sky. "Not today." He spoke with authority. "Just get 'otter. Tonight, mebbe. Tomorrow, sure. Got to get these 'ere chrysanths in 'afore it comes; they're good and sturdy to stand up to a storm, but they don't like bein' planted in mud."

I trusted his forecast. My umbrella stayed in the stand and I strolled across the Close with no raincoat.

"Aren't you going to get wet, Dorothy?"

Clarice was in the staff room ahead of me, hanging her yellow slicker on her peg and setting her umbrella quietly in the stand.

"Bob Finch says it won't rain until tonight at the earliest. I should think you'd boil in that oilskin thing, or plastic, or whatever it is."

"Oh. Yes, I suppose it is warm, but Archie thought I should wear it." She smiled a little, and there was something in her tone that made me look up.

"You're looking very nice today, Clarice. That pink blouse suits you. You must be feeling better."

"I'm quite all right. I told you I was. I—had a headache on Friday, that's all. Did you have a pleasant weekend?"

I told her all about the party, and she smiled again.

"It sounds rather exhausting in this heat. Archie and I enjoyed a quiet weekend at home." There was that tone of voice again. Satisfied? Happy? I couldn't quite put my finger on it, but at any rate, she didn't seem likely to throw a fit of the vapors this afternoon.

Which was just as well. We were worked off our feet; for once I was glad Barbara Dean was also helping. We found ourselves side by side straightening the stock in one of the few slack moments.

"I had occasion to call on Mr. Benson this weekend, Dorothy; he does not seem to be an entirely satisfactory person, so perhaps you were wise to consult Mr. Pettifer. I trust your tarpaulin is properly fixed in place; a storm is coming, and we don't want further damage before the repairs can be completed."

"It seems secure, thank you, Mrs.—er—Barbara." Lightning didn't strike me down, so I ventured further conversation. "By the way, I'm thinking of a little visit to your old haunts. Some friends from Sheffield want me to come see them; you're from there originally, aren't you?"

"Yes."

The monosyllable was not encouraging, but I persisted. "I don't suppose you know them—Colin and Gillian Davis? They're both at Hallam University; he teaches sculpture and she's in drama."

"I have very few contacts in Sheffield now. My family are all gone, and I have lived in Sherebury since I married, many years ago. Yes, sir, may I help you?"

And she turned to a customer, almost, I thought, with relief. But probably she was simply discouraging familiarity on the part of her inferior. And I'd thought we were beginning to be on equal terms. The nuances of English social relations still elude me.

Business slacked off at the end of the day, and Willie shooed me away a bit early. True to Bob's prediction, the storm hadn't broken by the time I got home, but it was nearer and I was as restless as the cats. I ate an unsatisfactory supper of leftovers and decided to call Alan. I wanted to tell him I was probably leaving town again for a few days, and he might also have some updated information. He wasn't home, though; I finally reached him at his office.

"No, nothing new. So far as I know." He sounded tired and distracted, and I could hear conversation in the background. "The trail's pretty cold by now, you know. Two weeks—Morrison reports to me only when there's some promising development. And we've had two serious drugs cases break over the weekend, and an armed robbery, and a smash-and-grab raid on the jewelers in the High Street. And of course The Visit." I could hear the capital letters even on the phone. "How was your weekend?"

"Fun. A little hectic. Alan, I won't keep you, but I'm thinking of paying a short visit to some friends in Sheffield. They've written, and I thought I might take it as an invitation. I just might find out something."

"It's a big place, Dorothy. I very much doubt that you'll learn anything to the purpose. In any case—damn, there's the other phone, and my secretary's gone home."

"I'll let you know when I'm leaving."

"Fine."

He'd hung up before he'd even finished the word.

Well! This was apparently my day for being rebuffed. He was busy, of course, and tired, but surely he could have been a little friendlier? Or had I just been imagining that his feelings for me were—I didn't want to pin down exactly what I'd thought about our relationship, but I was certainly confused. My restless energy suddenly collapsed in on itself like a dying star, leaving the same sort of black hole. Turning for comfort to a cat, I found that both of them had disappeared, probably under my bed, to wait out the approach of the storm. The sky was growing very dark, with an ominous greenish cast.

I turned on the lights and tried to think positively. I had other friends, after all. Friends who enjoyed my company. They'd said so. I picked up the phone again and punched in the lengthy series of numbers to reach Sheffield.

Colin answered on the second ring.

"Hello, Colin? It's Dorothy Martin."

"Well, hullo, love! Gill, it's Dorothy—pick up the other phone." He came back to me. "I can't hear you very well. Are you here in Sheffield?"

"No, I'm at home, and we're going to have a thunderstorm any minute. You're not very clear, either." I raised my voice and pressed the receiver to my ear. "Gillian, I got your note, and I really have been meaning to come up and see you. It's awfully short notice, but how would this coming weekend do?"

"Oh, but what a pity!" It was Gillian's voice, but it faded in and out. "We're just off to . . . tomorrow, for a fortnight. Colin . . . some sketches for a big bronze he's planning, and I'm . . . a play."

"Sorry, I missed some of that. You're off to where?"

"Portugal!" Colin's voice came through loud and clear for a

moment. "Why don't you come along with us, and we could have a good, long holiday?"

I tried to hide my disappointment. "It sounds delightful, and it's very kind of you to ask, but I can't. I've got too many irons in the fire here to be gone for more than a few days. Actually—oh, I might as well admit it. I was hoping to pick your brains about a—well, something puzzling that's happened here in Sherebury."

"About *what?*" said Gill. The line was getting worse.

"A murder," I shouted. We might be cut off at any moment; there wasn't time for circumlocution.

"There's a man here, a builder named Pettifer, who's from Sheffield originally. He's been trying to develop the Town Hall into a shopping mall, and there's a lot of controversy about it. Anyway, a couple of weeks ago a young man was found murdered in the Town Hall. His name was Jack Jenkins, and he was from Sheffield, too. And there's a third person involved, also from Sheffield—Pettifer's chief opposition, a formidable lady named Barbara Dean, head of the local preservation society. So you see, your part of the world plays rather a prominent role, and I wondered if any of those names rang a bell."

There was a crackly silence at the other end of the line, and thunder began to rumble close by.

"Did you get all that?" I asked anxiously.

"Most of it." Jack's voice sounded faint. "I can't say it raised any instant recognition in my mind. What about you, Gill?"

"None of the names, no," she said, and I thought I could hear doubt in her voice. "I do recall a scandal here a few years ago about a building controversy, if that might have a connection, but I don't think any of your people were involved."

It sounded awfully tenuous. "What was it about?"

The static began again in earnest as Colin and Gillian talked at once. "Council housing . . . blocks of flats . . . pensioners . . . fire . . . faulty wiring . . . three people died."

"Who was the contractor?" I shouted, afraid of the answer, but straining to hear. The rain had begun pelting down, and thunder boomed almost continuously. "Was it Archibald Pettifer?"

"No," said William, decisively, and for a moment clearly. "I'd remember a damn-fool name like that. No, it was about three years ago, and the names have vanished from my mind. I do remember the preservation faction was led by a woman, but then they nearly always are, aren't they? That's probably why Gill remembered at all—parallel with your case—but I've lost her name as well."

"Me, too," said Gillian, "but I do recall one rather poignant detail, now that I think of it. One of the people killed in the fire was her old auntie. The newspapers—"

There was a blinding flash of lightning and a doomsday crack of thunder. All my lights went out, and I was holding a dead telephone in my shaking hand.

The house hadn't been struck, I realized after a quick, terrified tour of inspection. It was the magnificent old oak tree between my house and Jane's. A large limb lay in my backyard, crushing all Bob's work in the flower beds, and incidentally burying electrical and phone wires. As the tempest raged and lightning flashed, I could see other trees straining before the wind.

It was a terrifying storm, but like most of its kind, it didn't last long. As soon as the rain slowed to a drizzle, I ran over to check on Jane—the front way. She popped out of her front door the same moment I did.

"Stay out of your back garden, Dorothy!" she shouted. "The cables are down!"

"I know. I was coming to tell you the same thing. I'm off to the nearest working telephone to report it."

I awoke late to a clear, balmy morning denying all connection with storm and tempest, and began to assess the damage.

Destruction was everywhere. Limbs had fallen from venerable old trees all over the neighborhood, in one case through a roof. My tarp had miraculously held, but the wind had driven rain under it and into my upstairs hall.

As I set out for my job, Bob stood mutely by my gate, unable to work with live wires everywhere, but shaking his head at the flood of mud and all the young plants that lay with roots miserably exposed, dying in the brilliant, crisp sunshine.

13

I WAS GREETED at the bookshop by a notice on the door announcing that, due to power failure, the shop was closed until further notice. As the only window in the place was so small as to admit almost no light anyway, the decision was practical, but I was annoyed that no one had let me know. Unreasonable, of course—how was anyone to phone me?—but I wasn't feeling reasonable. Upset with Alan, my nerves frayed by the storm and my abortive conversation with the Davises, I badly needed to talk to someone sensible. As usual, Jane was the chosen victim.

I dumped my purse in my kitchen and was heading out the door when I happened to glance at the calendar. It had a red ring around Tuesday, July 6. Today was Jane's birthday.

Oh, dear. I couldn't go over there without an offering of some sort. Jane might snort over whatever I brought and say it was all nonsense, one didn't have birthdays at her age, I should have had better sense—but she would be deeply hurt if I forgot. I picked up my purse and headed out again.

Almost without conscious volition, I found myself walking into Underwood's. A silly choice of shops, really; I'd never seen anything in Mavis's emporium to appeal to Jane's practical, earthy taste, and I knew from past experience that I'd almost certainly end up buying something. Perhaps my subconscious wanted to see how Mavis was doing.

Once I had seen, I had plenty of material for thought.

For Mavis was doing very well indeed. The shop, deserted the last time I'd been in, had five or six customers. A pretty young assistant was manning the cash register, while Mavis was showing the brass bedstead to a couple that looked likely to buy it.

I lurked in the back of the shop, fiddling with a pile of hearth rugs until Mavis had triumphantly negotiated the sale and noticed me.

"Good morning, Mrs. Martin," she trilled. "Lovely morning after the storm, isn't it?"

"A good day for cleaning up, and there's a lot of it to do. At least you have electricity, which is more than I can say. Did you have any damage at home?"

"I hadn't the time to notice, did I? Rushed myself off just to look in at the other shops before I fetched up here."

"You seem to be very busy today."

"My dear! I haven't had a moment to so much as sneeze these past few days. It's quite incredible."

The color in her cheeks today looked natural, and her hair had been toned up to an even brighter auburn. She glowed.

"It looks as though murder's been good for business, then, doesn't it? One can't always rely on how the public will react, I suppose."

Her eyes hardened. "I can't imagine what you mean, dear. Were you interested in those rugs? Lovely and thick, you see, they'll wear forever."

They weren't actually impossible. The roses were a trifle too large and a trifle too pink, but for keeping sparks off the carpet, they'd do. I picked one up, paid the exorbitant price, and walked out wondering with half my mind what on earth Jane was going to do with it, while the other half was busy considering the benefit Mavis had, unexpectedly, derived from the death of a twenty-three-year-old boy.

I found a ribbon in a crowded drawer in my kitchen, tied it around the rug, and marched next door, avoiding the workmen who were cautiously dealing with live wires in my erstwhile flower beds.

"Happy birthday," I said, thrusting the rug into Jane's arms as I stepped around a rush of eager, curious dogs. "If you hate it, take it to the next jumble sale or use it on the floor of one of the kennels. And for pity's sake, make me a cup of tea and let me talk to you."

Jane, being Jane, accepted that ungracious speech with no more than a raised eyebrow and established me at the kitchen table with tea and biscuits before she even untied the ribbon. Then she growled an utterly characteristic, deprecating thanks and sat down opposite me, head cocked inquiringly. "Problems?"

"Oh, I don't know! It's just—that was a really bad storm; it scared me. And I'm being snubbed by Barbara Dean—though that's hardly news—and Alan doesn't have time for me and some friends I wanted to visit are going away. In short, I'm feeling thoroughly sorry for myself. And I'm not getting anywhere with the murder, either."

Jane's eyes were calm, searching. "Why do you have to?"

"Well, of all the—do you want a murderer to go free? I thought the English cared more about justice than that!" My voice had risen; my hands waved in the air, and the nearest dog growled a small warning.

Jane's voice remained level. "We do. Why you?"

"What—oh." I felt suddenly very warm. "Sorry. I get carried away. It's a reasonable question, and I don't really know the answer. Except that this whole business seems to be connected with the question of preserving old buildings and—and good workmanship in general—and those are things I care about. And Alan is so busy—oh, I know he doesn't really have anything to do with day-to-day police work, but his men are all tied up with the royal visit, too, and they just don't seem to be doing anything. And besides—you didn't see him, Jane. That young kid, spread out there on the floor. I can't forget how pathetic he looked."

Jane looked at me searchingly over her teacup. "Can't leave well enough alone, can you?"

"I could," I retorted. "If anything were well enough. It isn't."

"Ah, well. You have a talent for landing on your feet. And as for Alan—he'll come round." She looked out the kitchen window. "Phone's probably working now—they've done with the wires."

I put my cup down. "Oh, then I'll get out of your way. I have a phone call to make."

I couldn't help it if she thought I was about to phone Alan.

In fact, he was not even on my list for today. I was definitely annoyed with Alan Nesbitt. If he wasn't interested in what I had to say, fine. No doubt he could get along perfectly well without my help, and I had no wish to intrude where I wasn't wanted. He obviously had better things to do with his precious time.

Which just goes to show how silly and spiteful a middle-aged woman can be.

My phone call was to Sheffield, or it was intended to be. I couldn't get through. Even though my phone was working fine, lines were evidently down all over the place, and circuits weren't available.

Well, I wasn't going to let that stop me. Probably the Davises were already on their way to Portugal, anyway. If I wanted more details about that building scandal that had begun to intrigue me, I'd have to look closer to home.

In the year I had lived in Sherebury, I'd become well acquainted with its excellent public library. I wasn't quite sure how to go about looking up an old news story, when I didn't know the date or the papers that might have covered it, but assuming the lights were on and the library open, someone, I was confident, would help me.

It was the reference librarian who showed me the microfilm machines and gave me a whole drawer full of the *Times*, as well as an index. I'd have to rely on the national papers; Sherebury, in the southeast, wasn't particularly interested in the affairs of a big city far to the northwest of it, and the library didn't carry their regional publication.

The search was less tedious than I'd supposed. In less than an hour I had my information, but I wasn't sure I knew much more than I had before. The fire that had destroyed a Sherebury apartment complex (a "block of flats"), built to house the elderly, had happened over three years ago, in March. It had been a late-breaking story; names of the victims were withheld pending notification of their families. The *Times* said there would be an investigation into the possibility that faulty wiring was to blame, but I couldn't find a follow-up article on the results of the investigation, nor did I see the names of the victims, presumably published later. The only other mention of the affair at all was a very brief news item a couple of years earlier, about the proposed project to be built by the firm of Mr. George Crenshawe & Co., which was arousing some opposition on the part of preservationists who felt the Victorian terrace and redundant church on the site should not be demolished. No members of the opposition were named. There was a picture of Mr. Crenshawe and a member of the county council, shaking hands and beaming.

I sighed. Really there seemed to be no connection with Sherebury at all. Peering again at the picture, squinting through the bottom of my bifocals, I could see that Mr. Crenshawe was a man, had the usual number of arms, legs, and eyes, and was bald. The photograph had never been especially good; microfilm reproduction hadn't improved it.

I decided to be thorough about the search while I was at it. Knowing the dates helped. I worked my way through the *Telegraph*, the *Guardian*, and the *Evening Standard* before deciding enough was enough. My neck had what felt like a permanent crick in it from the angle required to read a screen through bifocals, and I'd learned nothing really relevant. The *Standard*, given the benefit of a later deadline, did give the names and ages of those killed in the fire, and I dutifully copied them down. Miss Hattie Bulstrode, 83, Mrs. Janet MacLeod, a mere 76, and Mr. James Wyatt, 99. The last was particularly pathetic, since Mr. Wyatt's 100th birthday would have been in three days, and he was said to have been vigorous, active, and looking forward to the celebration.

Well, the *Standard* would have said that even if he'd been a feeble old man with little mind left. All girls are pretty in newspapers, all women at least striking, all victims pitiable. It makes better copy. Still, I left the library full of fury.

If I ever encountered Mr. George Crenshawe, he'd better watch out.

I spent the afternoon trying to help Bob restore some order to my desolate wreck of a garden. Working on my knees, getting mud on my hands and very nearly everywhere else, had the usual effect of restoring balance to my mind. Gardening is a steadying occupation; it's so very real.

So, after I'd scrubbed off the worst of the mud, I decided to relent and try to call Alan. I had no idea whether the pitiful little bits of information I'd gathered would be of interest, but he deserved to have them. It was simply silly to carry a pique, like a teenager.

He was, as I expected, at the office, and my high-minded mood didn't last long.

"Hello, Dorothy, I'm up to—hold on a moment." I could hear a brief, muted conversation at the other end of the line before he turned his attention back to me. "Sorry. As I started to say, things are a trifle frantic here. What can I do for you?"

"Well, there are some things I wanted to talk to you about, and I was hoping you might have time for a quick meal, but I don't suppose . . ." I trailed off disconsolately, but Alan, usually sensitive to my moods, didn't pick up on my tone of voice.

"Sorry, it's sandwiches from the canteen for me this evening. What's on your mind?"

His impatience was fully justified. He was plainly juggling a great many problems at once and didn't have time to deal with a dithering female.

Which didn't make me feel one bit better.

"It's nothing I can talk about on the phone. And probably not important, anyway. You're busy; I'll let you go."

This time he did catch it. "Dorothy, I—"

I hung up, gently.

14

T H E   T R O U B L E   W I T H   assertions of independence is that
they often feel fine at the time, but the warm self-righteousness
cools all too soon to a hard lump of misery. I spent the rest of
the evening wishing I hadn't hung up on Alan, or hadn't called
him at all, and forcing myself not to call again, and went to bed
missing Frank so fiercely I cried myself to sleep. For once, two
warm, friendly cats were no help at all.

Weary, red-eyed, and late, I dragged myself out of bed in
the morning and decided to go to the bookshop. Wednesday isn't
one of my regular days, but they might be deluged with tourists
after being closed for a day, and I felt I needed something pro-
ductive to do. My moods were becoming entirely too dependent
on one Alan Nesbitt.

When I got there I found everyone as edgy as I was. It was
another British Tourist Authority kind of day, warm and sunny,
so the place was full of customers clamoring for service, and
Mrs. Williamson—I *had* to remember to call her Willie—and
Barbara Dean were trying to cope by themselves with a busload
of camera-laden Japanese and another of earnest-looking Ger-
mans. I hurled myself into the fray, wishing I had some profi-

ciency in some language other than English (or, as the English would insist, American).

"Where's Clarice?" I hissed at Willie as I rang up seventeen postcards and she finished explaining that she really could not take traveler's checks written in yen, they'd have to be changed at a bank. "We need her."

"Don't know," she said, pawing frantically through a pile of illustrated cathedral guidebooks for the German-language version. "Home, I suppose. She hasn't phoned and I haven't had a moment to ring her or talk to Barbara. She might know, if you can catch her; it was late Monday afternoon, after you left, when Clarice collapsed again and had to be taken home. Here you are, sir, that's one pound fifty."

"*Bitte?*" said the elderly man, studying his handful of heavy English coins with a puzzled frown.

Willie managed a smile, though it was a little frayed around the edges, and began to sort through the coins for the ones she needed. "See, this thick one is a pound, and this is ten pence . . ."

But Clarice had been in such a good mood Monday! I didn't understand at all, but there was no time to think about it until a lull hit a couple of hours later, and I made a pot of tea. Barbara Dean came into the staff room to join me, looking more human than I'd ever seen her. Her hair wasn't perfect and there was actually a smudge on her lapel. She sat down heavily in the squashy old armchair and accepted a cup of tea with murmured thanks.

"You look tired, Barbara," I ventured, settling gingerly on the couch, which was easier to get into than out of.

She sighed, and then pulled herself together. "So do you," she said, "and we've both earned it. We should all have been a great deal better off this morning with more help."

That gave me my opening. "Yes, what's the matter with Clarice, do you know? Mrs.—Willie said she caved in again on Monday."

"I'm afraid I haven't the slightest idea," Barbara said crisply. "We were simply talking when she turned white as paper and crumpled. Canon Richards took her home."

"Good heavens. Was it something about the murder again, do you think? She's awfully sensitive about that, for some reason. I think she's still worried that her husband might be—suspected."

"If that is the case, she ought to have been reassured. Yes, we were discussing the matter, but quite calmly. I told her I was quite certain that the roots of the matter lay with the boy's background, in Sheffield. And she fainted dead away."

"But that makes no sense at all. Do you think she's ill?"

Barbara shrugged, and I took a different tack.

"I'm curious, though. There was a building scandal in Sheffield not too long ago—well, you probably know all about it. Do you think it could possibly have anything to do with our murder?"

"I'm afraid I prefer not to talk about Sheffield. There are some rather painful memories . . ." There was a surge of noise, and Barbara put down her teacup and stood up. "There seems to be quite a crowd coming in again. Perhaps we should get back to work."

Well, that was a clear "No Trespassing" sign. But she'd talked about Sheffield to Clarice. Was it because I was a foreigner, or had I said something wrong somehow? I was going to have to be very careful with future questions, at any rate. Not sure of an approach, I wasn't really sorry I had no more chance to speak to Barbara until the end of the morning, which was when the really odd thing happened.

Lunchtime had thinned out the crowd, and all three of us, Barbara, Willie, and I, had seized the chance to tidy up. Barbara and I were working together at a shelf of poetry that had been wildly disarranged, and I was making conversation, trying to work my way back to Sheffield, when she suddenly stood stock-still, staring at the book in her hand. I had never seen such a look on anyone's face. She might have been a Greek goddess, or one of the Fates—cold, implacable marble.

"Barbara, is something wrong? Are you okay?"

"What?" Her voice came from a great distance. "Oh. Yes. Please excuse me." And she put the book on the shelf, precisely where it belonged, and walked out of the shop, stopping only to pick up her handbag.

I stared after her, and then picked up the book she had been holding.

What on earth was there about the poems of George Herbert to turn anyone to stone?

I STAYED MOST of the afternoon. Even with the two women of the afternoon shift, we were frantically busy until after four, when the weather changed and the flood of tourists diminished to a trickle, and Willie shooed me out. "You've done a yeoman's job, and I'm truly grateful, but it's time you put your feet up. You look tired."

I was, in fact, exhausted after a restless night and hours of standing, and nothing sounded better than putting my feet up and having a cup of tea. Or perhaps something stronger. However, duty called, and resentfully I listened. I should stop at Clarice's to see how she was. The woman could be infuriating, but she was a friend, and friendship shouldn't be taken lightly.

The gray sky and gentle sound of the rain were most conducive to a nap. I knew if I once relaxed, I was out for the count. So I hurried home, getting wet in the process, greeted the cats, had a cup of tea, and climbed into the car. Maybe I could find out what was bothering the wretched woman, anyway.

Once I got to her house, with no more than the usual number of wrong turns, I thought I might have saved myself the trouble. Clarice wasn't talking and didn't appreciate my solicitude. She let me in with a reluctance that was downright insulting, though she tried to disguise it, and sat nervously on the very edge of one of the blocky modern couches in the living room.

"It's very good of you to come, I'm sure, but Archie will be home in a moment and I really must—"

She tried to think what she really must do while I assessed her. Her hair was in strings, her face, blotchy from crying, was innocent of makeup, and her frilly blue blouse and brown-and-orange tweed skirt didn't go together. Balled up in one hand was a damp handkerchief which the other hand picked at.

"You're very kind, but I—I have a bit of a headache, and—"

I could stand it no longer. "Clarice, I can well believe you have a headache, but there's a lot more to it than that. You're a wreck. I've never seen you like this. Is it Archie?"

She looked terrified. "No! No, of course not! There's nothing wrong with Archie—he—I have a headache, that's all."

"You're on the verge of a nervous breakdown," I said flatly. I had lost my patience. "When will your husband be home?"

"Soon. You mustn't—"

"I intend to see to it that you're looked after, since he doesn't seem to be doing a very good job. Clarice, you must see that you need help. You've been falling apart ever since that wretched murder—"

She went even whiter than before and slid off the couch to the floor as Mr. Pettifer walked into the room.

"May I ask," he said with cold fury, "precisely why you are bullying my wife?"

"Bullying! I'm trying to—we can't stand here arguing, she's fainted, she needs—"

"I believe I am the best judge of what she needs. You will have the goodness to leave my house, Mrs. Martin!" He turned his back on me, picked up Clarice with a strength I hadn't known he possessed, laid her on the couch, and began chafing her wrists.

"But—she needs a doctor, I could—"

"Get out!" It was a stage whisper, with the effect of a roar. I got out.

And just what, I thought as I drove slowly down the wrong side of the fortunately deserted street, was that all about? Was she afraid of Archie? Did he beat her, after all? If so, he was careful to make sure it didn't show; her face was a mess, but it wasn't bruised. He certainly had a temper, but he had treated her gently when he'd picked her up, and only two days ago she had acted—well, to tell the truth, she'd acted like a teenager in love, mooning about Archie, making excuses to bring his name into the conversation.

Was she afraid *for* him? I was sure she'd had suspicions all along that he was involved in the Town Hall murder. That could explain her behavior. Suppose Archie had managed somehow to convince her that he was in the clear, and then—yes! And then Barbara Dean said something to her that awakened her suspicions with more force than ever! Hence her collapse. It would have to be something to do with Sheffield. Was Archie the crooked contractor after all? And why wouldn't Barbara talk to me about Sheffield?

The blare of a horn shocked me back onto my side of the road, where I promptly stalled the engine and sat for a moment, quivering. When my mind began to function again, I realized the Archie-as-criminal-contractor theory wouldn't fly. He'd left Sheffield far too long ago. But logically, Barbara Dean must have said *something* to send Clarice into a tailspin. Well, why not ask her again?

I peered out the car windows; I'd been driving more or less aimlessly for a few minutes while my thoughts were racing after an explanation. Sherebury isn't a big town, but it can be confusing, and I wasn't sure quite where I was. The Pettifers live in an exclusive development, all cul-de-sacs and curves, which adjoins a lovely old neighborhood with even more narrow, curvy streets and complicated hills.

There was something familiar about the area, though. Surely

I'd been here before? These houses looked familiar. The big stone one, especially—

The big stone one was Barbara Dean's house. I'd been there only once, to a genteel sort of tea party for the bookshop volunteers, but I was certain.

Almost certain, at least. I got out of the car. There was no harm in ringing the bell. If it was the wrong house, I could apologize, go home, and phone the blasted woman. If I was right, she could hardly refuse to let me in, and it was just possible I could extract some information.

I rang.

And rang once more.

And waited.

The rain was setting in hard now, and obviously no one was home. Of course, Barbara was a widow and lived alone. If this was even her house. I gave up, splashed back to my car, and drove off, peering anxiously past the monotonous swish of the windshield wipers. After three random turns, I had no idea at all where I was. It wasn't yet six, but the clouds were so dark and the rain so heavy I could see very little. There wouldn't be a soul on the street in this downpour; asking directions was out.

Maybe if I tried to head downhill? That at least would bring me to the main body of the town, and with luck to a street I recognized. How lost could one get, for heaven's sake, in a town the size of Sherebury?

Very lost.

The last straw was when I slithered down a steep, nasty little cobbled lane, took the sharp turn at the bottom too fast, and came to a shuddering stop a couple of feet from the edge of the riverbank.

That scared some sense into me. There was no point in my continuing to drive aimlessly in this weather. If I had to, I could walk home. At least I knew where the river was, though I wasn't familiar with this part of it. I must be on the very edge of town, even if I wasn't certain whether it was the east or the west edge. I abandoned the car to its wildly unsuitable and probably illegal parking spot and set out, umbrella-less, to seek help.

And there, looming out of the rain and put there by all the saints, was a pub, a large, well-known riverside pub that was supposed to have good food. Then this was the Lanterngate area, to the west, and only five minutes from the High Street. Well, no matter that I now knew where I was and where home was; I was tired and wet and hungry, and I made for the sign of the King's Head like a homing pigeon.

" 'Struth, madam, been out for a dip in the river, have you, then?"

I dripped copiously on the flagstone floor as I walked into the bar and cast bitter glances at the stone-cold hearth. "No," I answered the barman through chattering teeth. "Just a dip in your lovely English climate. Is there someplace where I could dry off a bit, do you think?"

"Sarah!" he bellowed through a doorway, and a comfortable-looking woman bustled in, a white apron around her ample waist. "Sarah, love, take the lady upstairs and get her dry. Here you are, dear." This was to me, as he handed me a balloon glass with something amber in it. "Keep the cold out. On the house."

"Oh, dear, dear, dear," murmured Sarah. "You look like a drowned kitten, you poor thing. You come right through with me."

The King's Head, it seemed, was an inn as well. Sarah, presumably the innkeeper's wife, led me up steep, narrow stairs to a small room with a sloping floor and chintz curtains, and switched on the electric space heater that stood forlornly in a large fireplace.

"Now just you get out of those wet things, dear, and here are towels and a bathrobe. I'll have to bring you something of my own to wear whilst we dry your clothes in the kitchen."

"But—I'm not spending the night, you know. I just came in for a meal—"

"That'll be all right, dear. Don't worry. You're American, aren't you?"

I admitted it.

"Well, we can't have a visitor getting pneumonia, can we? Whatever would you think of us? Now you just drink your brandy and warm yourself at that nice electric fire and I'll be back in a tick."

"No, I do appreciate this, but I actually live in town, just at the other end, near the Cathedral. I should go home, really, I can't—"

Sarah put her hands on her hips and studied me. "Of course, dear! You're Mrs. Martin, aren't you? I didn't recognize you, with your hair all streaming. Now, you're not getting any younger, dear, if you don't mind my saying so. I couldn't rest easy, letting you go back out in the wet, cold through as you are. You'll have a nice meal, won't you, and your own things will dry and you'll go home feeling much better. You just leave things to me."

I gave in gratefully, Sarah bustled out, and I was glad to strip to my underwear, dry myself on the rough towels, and slip into the thick terry-cloth robe. I was warming my hands in front of the heater when she came back with an armful of clothes.

"Here you are, dear. The dress'll be big on you, but it has a belt, and I've brought you a nice cardi to keep you warm."

I slipped into the navy blue dress and white cardigan sweater.

"There now!" said my rescuer delightedly. "That isn't so bad, after all!"

"It's wonderful," I said sincerely. "This is so very kind of you, and I don't even know your name—except Sarah."

"Sarah Hawkins. My husband and I own this place; he's Derek, down in the bar." She shook hands, the formal gesture seeming a little odd from someone who had seen me in my skivvies a moment before.

"Well, Mrs. Hawkins, I certainly owe you a great favor. Now about that meal—do you really have room for one more for dinner? I'm sure you're busy."

"We are that," she said with satisfaction. "If you wouldn't mind sharing a table? There's one of our residents dining alone, and he never minds a bit of company. You'll find him a very pleasant gentleman, friendly, but not—you know." She cocked her eyebrows to indicate that I was safe from molestation, and I grinned.

"Sounds fine to me."

I was settled at a table for two, my brandy had been topped up, and I had ordered a substantial meal before I had cause to change my mind. I was scrabbling in my purse for a tissue when a familiar voice made me look up.

"Well, well, what a pleasant surprise! Our good hostess told me I was to have a dinner companion, but she didn't mention your name. Doing well, are you, Mrs. Martin, eh?"

Herbert Benson clapped me on the shoulder with a heavy, ringed hand, scraped back his chair, put down his large glass of gin, and sat down, beaming all the way to the edge of his bright-brown hair.

15

THERE WAS NO help for it. Mr. Benson might not be my favorite person, but I could scarcely stalk out of the King's Head in a downpour, wearing someone else's clothes. I was stuck.

"Why, Mr. Benson," I said with as much charm as I could muster, "I had no idea you were staying here. I would have thought you'd have found a house. How long have you been living in Sherebury, then?"

"Few months. To tell the truth, I've been too busy to look for a place of my own, and the Hawkinses do me very well here." He waved the matter away and went straight to the issue I wanted to avoid. "How're you getting on with your roof?"

My soup was served just then, which gave me an excuse for a brief reply. "Well, the tarp keeps the house more or less dry, and I have hopes the grant applications may be approved soon."

"Ah, well." He made a large gesture. "You'd have done better to leave it to me, you know. But—" He waved his right hand airily again and one of his rings slipped from his finger, clattering to the table. He put it back on and continued without missing a beat. "No harm done, and no offense taken, I'm sure. No need for you to worry about that!"

What chutzpah! He'd neatly turned his irresponsibility into my transgression—and then forgiven me for it! Torn between irritation and admiration, I concentrated on my soup.

"I'm afraid I won't have the time to take on those windows we talked about," he went on.

Well, thank goodness for that, anyway. Clearly I was no match for this man. If he'd decided he wanted to oversee the rest of my renovations, I'd not only have ended up with plastic windows, but been convinced they were what I wanted.

"I'm on to quite a good thing, actually," he went on. "Set to build those new blocks of flats for Pettifer. You've heard about them, I'm sure, going to pull down the old Victorian terraces near the university, not that they'll need much pulling down, ready to fall down by themselves, and put up nice new flats, modern, convenient . . ."

Ugly, I thought. But, looked at with the dispassionate eye I was trying to cultivate, the old ones weren't all that beautiful, either. Old and quaint, but dilapidated. Perhaps Pettifer was right, and they should be replaced. At any rate, Benson, with his love of modernity, was probably more safely employed on new buildings. However . . .

"Oh, yes? I'm surprised you're involved in that project, Mr. Benson." It was catty, but I felt I had the right to a lick or two. "Somehow I got the impression you and Mr. Pettifer were—not on very good terms. And surely his own men don't have enough to do right now. Why would he hire someone else to take over the job for him?"

My soup bowl was replaced by a plate of sausage, lamb chop, steak, bacon, liver, mushrooms, tomato—loaded with fat and cholesterol, and smelling wonderful.

"Oh, Archie and I are good friends, you know," Benson said, finishing his gin. "Here, waiter, I'll have the mixed grill as well, and we'll share a bottle of Australian claret, eh, Mrs. Martin?" He beamed at me. "No, we may quarrel from time to time, as old friends do, but when we can see it in our way to do the other a favor, we do it. There's too much between us for us not to be friends, you see."

The last remark made me look up sharply. There was more than a hint of a nudge-and-wink in Benson's voice, and an unmistakable leer on his face.

"What *do* you mean?"

My tone would have frozen an unruly fourth-grader back in my teaching days, but Benson was beginning to feel his gin, and took no notice.

"Ah, well, no need to spell it out to a clever lady like yourself, is there? We've all got our little secrets, haven't we? I daresay Archie has one or two things up his sleeve that he'd just as soon didn't get known, eh? An indiscretion or two in his past? That boy in the Town Hall, now. I fancied he had quite a look of—but least said soonest mended, eh? Here, now, you're not drinking your wine!"

"I don't care very much for red wine," I lied. Actually I didn't care very much for Benson's increasing inebriation, nor for his innuendos.

"What a pity—you ought to've told me. Would you prefer white? Or a nice glass of beer, or—"

"No, thank you." Probably he meant well, I thought, trying to be charitable. "It's very kind of you, but I really don't want anything more to drink. I didn't get a lot of sleep last night, and I don't like to drink much when I'm driving anyway. The English laws—" I stopped. Why was I explaining so elaborately?

Benson leaned forward earnestly. "Ah, now, y'see, that's your trouble. You let the law intimidate you. Planning laws, traffic laws. The way I look at it is, see, the law's your servant. Who had the idea of laws to protect us in the first place? The common people, that's who. Magna Carta and all that, the common people against the king. It's even called common law, isn't it? But now they have their laws here and their laws there and they're all to put you under, keep you in your place. If a man's to look out for himself, he has to find the way to get round them, thass all." He burped. " 'Scuse me."

Taking out a cigarette, he put it between his lips, struck a match, and paused, fractionally. "Don't mind if I smoke, do you?"

"Yes, I do mind, as a matter of fact."

He had already taken a long drag. He looked at me in astonishment and choked on the lungful of smoke that was seeping out of his open mouth. I looked pointedly at the cigarette; he extinguished it, carefully, and slipped it back into the packet in his shirt pocket.

"Always happy t'oblige a lady," he said cheerfully, and I was hard put not to roll my eyes to the ceiling. Just once I would like to catch the man out, put him in the wrong so firmly that he would be forced to apologize, but he seemed unable even to recognize his own sins, much less repent them. I hoped his shirt caught fire.

"You're sure you won't have a li'l wine?"

"I'm sure." I was crisp. It had no effect whatever.

"Making a mistake, you know. S'nothing like a nice glass of wine, and this stuff's very nice indeed."

He poured the rest of the bottle into his glass and his left hand caressed it, fat little fingers looking like sausages with rings tightly embedded in the flesh. His sibilants were beginning to hiss a trifle more than he intended.

" 'S'matter of fact, this was what I was drinking the night—the night of that meeting, you know. Good old Derek's got quite a lot of it laid down, 's good stuff. . . ."

He was more than a little tight, and I didn't like the way he was leaning toward me. "That would have been the night of the murder, wouldn't it?" I said hurriedly. "When Mr. Pettifer was with you, after the meeting?"

He looked at me with owlish solemnity. "Couldn' deceive a

lady, now could I? Don't like to let down a pal, but mush—mussen lie to a lady. Lie to the police. Don' like the poleesh. Laws, intid—timin—out to get you." He finished his wine in one large gulp and began to sing. "All alone—I'm so all alone—" He broke off. "Can't remember resh of wordsh. Alone. All alone. 'Scuse me."

He got up with careful dignity and walked in the direction of the stairway, wavering only slightly, but causing raised eyebrows as he passed. Mrs. Hawkins, drawn by the singing, came over to me, flustered.

"Oh, dear, I'm so sorry, Mrs. Martin! I've never seen the poor man like that before. I suppose he was being convivial and lost count. Are you quite all right?"

"Yes, thank you. It's certainly not your fault. It's been a long day, though, and I'm ready to drop. Are my clothes dry, do you think?"

"I'm afraid they're still quite damp. Why don't you just wear that dress home? It's too tight for me, you know, so I shan't be wanting it till I can slim a bit." She sighed, running her hands down her hips. "But our cook is so good—did you enjoy your dinner? You'll have your sweet, won't you, and some coffee to buck you up? It's still raining."

I was too tired to resist, even if I'd wanted to. I did as she suggested, left when the rain finally stopped, and managed to find my way home before sleep caught up with me and blotted everything out.

THE NEXT MORNING the world was soft and foggy, with sounds and sights muffled and misty, a perfect day to roll over and go back to sleep. I wasn't allowed to, of course. Last night I'd heartlessly closed the bedroom door against my four-legged alarm clocks, but the instant they heard me move they'd bounded up the stairs to my door and stayed, creating various sound effects designed to speed up breakfast. Esmeralda has perfected a door-pounding method, standing on her hind legs and battering very quickly with alternate front paws. It's similar to a scratching-post routine except with retracted claws, and with her considerable weight behind those powerful legs, it's extremely effective on the loose-fitting old door. *Bam bam bam bam bam* . . . endlessly.

Samantha, of course, has her Siamese wail.

I endured half an hour of it before dragging myself out of bed in martyrly fashion, afflicted with a headache and what my grandmother used to call "the rheumatics," my reward for getting soaked to the skin the day before.

My brain wasn't working very well either, I realized as I brooded over a cup of coffee. A confused mass of ideas thrashed about, refusing to form a coherent whole or even settle down long enough to be looked at intelligently. Sheffield, Barbara Dean, William Farrell, Archie Pettifer, the Town Hall, Clarice, Benson's nasty hints—I reached for a pad and put it down again drearily. I didn't have the energy to make a list.

What I needed was to talk to someone who knew all the details of the murder and could help me sort it out, see if some pattern would emerge.

What I needed was Alan.

I looked at the phone, and then looked away. I'd gotten over my temper, but common sense told me there was no point in trying to reach the chief constable three days before a royal visit. Even if he was in, he was likely to be barricaded behind a wall of secretaries, and in no mood to talk. I might be able to reach him this evening, talk him into a late dessert, but that was hours from now.

So, failing Alan, I was on my own. Even Jane hadn't been all that sympathetic; she clearly thought I should mind my own business.

Three aspirin and two cups of coffee later I reached for the phone. As my headache faded (replaced by heartburn), I'd remembered I wanted to talk to Barbara Dean. This time I intended to be direct. I couldn't spend the rest of my life in terrified awe of the woman, and I needed some answers. Why did she think Sheffield was at the heart of a Sherebury murder? Did it have anything to do with the Sheffield building scandal? I was sorry if she didn't want to talk about it, but I was tired of playing games by other people's rules. I intended to ask about Pettifer's past, too. Much as I hated to put any stock in Benson's hints, they might be relevant.

I punched in the number briskly and let the phone ring at least twenty times before I dropped the receiver back on the cradle.

So that, too, would have to wait. Frustrated, but doggedly stubborn, I reached again for the pad and pencil.

A half hour of intense concentration produced only a brief list of not very brilliant questions in no particular order.

THINGS I WANT TO FIND OUT

1. What, if anything, does Sheffield have to do with our murder?
2. Who were the preservationists in that battle?
3. Why doesn't Barbara want to talk about it?
4. What on earth is the matter with Clarice?
5. Is there anything to Benson's hint about Jack Jenkins being Archie's son?
6. Was Benson really with Archie the night of the murder?

And I couldn't think of a single answer.

After trying Barbara again, I gave it up and headed next door, praying Jane would be home. If she didn't want to talk, she might at least have some idea where I could find Barbara. (I was beginning to be able to think of her by her first name, I congratulated myself. Another year or two and I might get comfortable with it.)

I negotiated Jane's slippery back path, but before I could knock, a confusion of dogs leapt out the door, whining and barking and turning themselves inside out in their eagerness for a walk. They approached me for a ritual snuffle, but immediately turned their attention back to Jane, following with three leashes in hand.

"Uh-oh!" I shouted over the commotion. "Bad timing! I was coming to see you, but I don't dare delay the troops, do I?"

"Come along with us," Jane roared. "QUIET, dogs!" The clamor decreased by a decibel or two and she shrugged. "They'll shut up once we're on our way."

We made for a vacant lot a few streets away, covered with rank grass and weeds, and much favored by dog owners. There Jane turned the dogs loose to run as they wished, and we sank onto a wooden bench whose surface was beaded with water.

"Jane, I must confess I have an agenda. Do you have any idea where I might reach Barbara Dean? I really need to talk to her, and she doesn't seem to be home."

She sat up a little straighter and looked at me. "Second person today to ask me that. Don't know why everyone thinks I'm the information bureau." But it was said without rancor. She knew perfectly well why, really; she almost always had the answers.

"Mayor rang up this morning," she went on. "Or his secretary did. Dean missed a meeting last night. Preservation Society. Didn't send word. Mayor was speaking, everyone upset she wasn't there."

My eyes widened. "But, Jane, she's chairman of the Preservation Society!"

"Mmm." Her eyes turned back to the dogs.

"And she wasn't home yesterday, either, at least early in the evening, because I knocked on her door about—oh, six, probably. I thought she'd gone out to dinner. I could have been mistaken about the house, but I don't think I was. And I've been calling all morning, on the phone, I mean, and there's been no answer. Do you think we should check on her? She—I suppose she could have fallen . . . or something . . ." My voice trailed away doubtfully. Somehow, the vision of Barbara Dean as the helpless victim of an accident wasn't easy to conjure up; she was so totally competent, so utterly in control.

But Jane was frowning. "Not like her to be irresponsible. Never missed a meeting that I know of."

And Jane would know.

I looked at Jane, unease beginning to stir, and Jane looked at me and came to a decision. She stood and whistled for the dogs.

"Probably nothing wrong, but can't hurt to find out. Come along, dogs, better walkies later." They came, slowly, and allowed their leashes to be clipped on, voicing their disappointment and bewilderment all the way home.

Jane made one more attempt on the phone, letting it ring until it disconnected itself, and we sat there looking at each other.

"Jane, do you think . . . ?"

"Yes. I'll drive."

"Thank God," I said fervently.

I had driven around, lost, for at least half an hour last night; Jane found the house in five minutes. It was the right house, the house I'd tried, but there was still no sign of life. No lights were on, though the day was dull enough to need them. No one answered the door.

"Do you suppose the neighbors—?" I asked very tentatively. If Barbara had simply gone away on short notice, she would not appreciate our making a fuss about it.

Jane was made of sterner stuff, and had the bit between her teeth. "Not like her at all," she said stubbornly. "Something wrong. You take that side."

She set out for the houses to the right while I went to the left.

Some of the neighbors weren't home, but the ones immediately to either side, interrupted in the middle of their lunches, had no knowledge of Dean's being away, and expressed astonishment that she had failed to show up for a scheduled appointment. "But she'd never do such a thing!" was the universal opinion.

It was the man who lived directly across the street who was helpful. "You could check her car," he suggested. "She garages it just round the corner, where I put mine, as well." Certainly he would show us the way. He'd just tell his wife he'd be a moment—

"Each door has its own padlock, you see," he explained as we walked to the corner. "But it's one big building, and the individual bays are divided only by partitions, half height, rather like horse stalls, eh? Mrs. Dean keeps her car just next to mine, so we can easily see—ah, here we are."

The building was little more than a shed, flimsily built of wood, probably designed for some other purpose originally. But the enterprising owner, seeing profit in the ever-growing, desperate need for a place to park, had turned it into a five-bay garage with just enough space for the owner of each car to park it and squeeze out. The obliging neighbor pulled open the double doors of his bay and stepped inside. We didn't have to follow him; from the doorway we could see the car in the next bay.

Spotless, smug, uncommunicative, it sat there. Jane did manage to slide her bulk between the neighbor's car and the partition wall long enough to peer into Dean's car and then slide out again.

"Nothing," she said briefly.

There, behind firmly padlocked doors, was Barbara Dean's car, cold and empty. Where, then, was Barbara Dean?

16

"ALAN, I HAVE to see you."

I'd been doing a lot of serious worrying. It was clear that Barbara knew a lot more about the Sheffield end of this story than she had told anyone. What if she knew too much—knew for certain that the builder of those council flats was responsible for the fire? If the preservation people in Sheffield were her friends, as seemed likely, she'd be bitter about the deaths, particularly of the "old auntie."

Or, the thought had suddenly hit me, what if she'd been involved herself, and it was *her* aunt who had been killed? She'd said something about painful memories. And suppose, just suppose, that the builder in question, George Crenshawe, was in Sherebury?

It had taken me ages to reach Alan. His regular secretary wasn't in, and the substitute answering his calls was new and extremely protective. When she finally gave him my message and he finally called me back, I'd been pacing the floor for nearly an hour.

"What is it?" he asked, his voice sharp. "Sergeant Rogers didn't say your message was urgent—are you in trouble? Why didn't you ring my private number?"

"Samantha ate it," I said sourly. "She chewed off the whole bottom corner of my little address book. Look, there are a lot of things I don't want to discuss on the phone. Barbara Dean, and Clarice Pettifer, and the murder. And I do realize you're frantically busy, but this is important, Alan. Can't you take a break for tea?"

"Impossible. I'm off to London in an hour, with two hours' work to do before I go. If this is about the murder, I'll put you through to Morrison." Without giving me a chance to reply, he put the phone down. There was a series of clicks and buzzes and then the officious secretary came on the line.

"I'm sorry, Mrs. Martin, Inspector Morrison is not in the office. He'll ring you as soon as we can reach him."

"Oh, no, that's too much trouble, I don't want—"

"No trouble at all, Mrs. Martin." She hung up.

The tears in my eyes were due entirely to frustration. I was still trying to convince myself of that when the phone rang. Well, apologies weren't going to get him anywhere this time. I'd teach him to toy with my affections, I'd—I picked up the phone.

"Yes?" I hissed, trying to sound like Judith Anderson's Mrs. Danvers.

"Mrs. Martin? This is Inspector Morrison. The chief constable just rang me up, said you had some important information for me. He's frightfully sorry he can't deal with it himself, of course, but he asked if I'd pop round to see you. Would now be convenient?"

"Oh." I sounded as deflated as I felt. "Oh—uh—yes, that's fine. I live right next to the Cathedral Close, you know, at the end of Monkswell Street, you have to go up the High Street and turn left, and then—"

"I think I can find it, Mrs. Martin." His tone was carefully not amused. "I'll be there in ten minutes, then."

The interval was exactly long enough for me to set out tea, while feeling fifteen kinds of a fool. For calling a busy policeman out on what might well be a wild-goose chase, for venturing to give him directions, I, an American who had lived here for less than a year . . .

He was very nice about it.

"I hope you really don't mind my coming round on such short notice," he began when I had established him in a comfortable chair, "but the chief was quite insistent. He said if you thought something was important, it was, and we must sort it out immediately. He did ask me to send his apologies, by the way." He grinned in a friendly sort of way, becoming instantly much more human. "I was to tell you he's ready to do murder himself, either to a certain royal personage or to his staff—I quote verbatim—and he hopes you'll forgive him for being a trifle—er—preoccupied."

Preoccupied wasn't quite the way I would have put it, but I wasn't going to carry on my quarrel with Alan through an intermediary. "It just means you'll get his tea, though perhaps he isn't missing much; it's all out of tins. I haven't had much time to bake."

"I'm quite fond of chocolate biscuits, actually," said the inspector, helping himself to four. "However, I mustn't waste your time. The chief said you mentioned Barbara Dean and Pettifer. Is there a connection there we've missed?"

"I don't know." I poured him a cup of tea and adjusted my mind back to business, and suddenly felt much less apologetic. There really was something odd going on. "What I do know is this: There was a very messy affair in Sheffield some years ago." I told him the story I had pieced together from what the Davises had told me and my own researches, including my suppositions about Barbara Dean.

"Now, obviously, there's no proven connection with Sherebury there, but I'm convinced Mrs. Dean knows quite a lot about it. She's been saying the oddest things. In fact, she said something to Clarice Pettifer on Monday that upset her almost to the point of a nervous breakdown. She—Mrs. Dean, I mean—said she told Clarice the key to the murder must lie in Sheffield. And that brings me to the real point. I'm sure you wondered if I was eventually going to have one."

Morrison merely smiled.

"I've been trying for the best part of twenty-four hours now to reach Barbara Dean and ask her about all this. And—this is going to sound melodramatic, but I can't help it—she seems to be missing."

The inspector put down his teacup and gave me his full attention. "Exactly what do you mean by 'missing'?"

"Oh, not what the police mean officially, I suppose," I said a little impatiently. "I know there's something about forty-eight hours before they—you—will do anything."

"It depends upon the circumstances," Morrison said grimly. "Please go on."

"Well, she hasn't been seen, apparently, since yesterday around noon. There was a meeting of the Preservation Society— the *Preservation Society*, Inspector, she's the chairman, for heaven's sake—last night, and she neither showed up nor canceled. And she wasn't home sick, either, at least not around six, because I was at her house trying to find her. Anyway she was perfectly well when she left the bookshop just before lunch. A bit strange in manner, but in good health. And today she doesn't answer her phone, or her doorbell, but—and this is the worst part—her car is in the garage. Jane Langland and I checked. Now, doesn't that all sound to you like she's missing?"

"It warrants following up." Morrison swallowed the last bite of biscuit and and took out his notebook. "Now, what do you mean exactly by saying Dean was 'strange in manner' yesterday?"

"Well—preoccupied. She got that look on her face, as if she'd suddenly seen something in her mind. In cartoons they put a lightbulb over the head. You know, 'Eureka'?"

He nodded, with a small grin.

"Only this didn't seem to be a very pleasant thing, because I remember thinking she looked for a moment as if she'd been turned to stone. And then she put the book back on the shelf and just left, without a word of explanation or good-bye or anything."

"What book?"

"Oh, sorry. Just a book of poems. By George Herbert. I remember that because it seemed so dull and harmless."

The inspector stood up. "I'm very much obliged to you, Mrs. Martin, for letting us know about this right away. I'll set the machinery in motion, and let you know what progress we make in locating Mrs. Dean."

"Wait, there's more! I'll try not to take any more time than I have to, but you should know what Mr. Benson said to me last night about Mr. Pettifer."

"Ah, yes, Pettifer." The inspector sat down again.

"I had dinner with Benson last night, you see. Quite by accident; the King's Head was crowded and we had to share a table. I was tired, so he did most of the talking—and he said a lot, one way and another.

"I wish I could remember his exact words, because none of this was what you could call a definite statement; it was all in the way he looked and sounded. Innuendo, you know, nudges and winks and knowing looks. I hate that sort of thing, and I may have inferred all the wrong meanings. And to be honest, he'd had quite a lot too much to drink, so none of it may be very reliable. But what it boiled down to, if not in so many words, was a strong hint that Jack Jenkins was Mr. Pettifer's illegitimate son. He as much as said that the two of them looked alike, and that Mr. Pettifer had some dire secrets in his past."

"Really." The inspector tilted his head to one side and pursed his lips.

"I thought that might interest you. And what may be of even

more interest, although this was when he was really under the weather, was that he almost admitted he was lying about Pettifer being with him the night of the murder."

The inspector whistled softly.

"Now I could be all wet, as I said. And you won't forget he was drunk, will you? I don't pretend I have any fondness for Benson, but I'd hate for a man's ramblings to be held against him. I just thought you might want to talk to Benson yourself. You see, I can't help wondering if Pettifer might have had something to do with the fire in the Sheffield council flats."

"Perhaps. At any rate, yes, we'd like a little chat with Mr. Benson. If you're even close to the right interpretation, he has some explaining to do. Why didn't he come to us with all this?"

"He said he didn't like the police. He seems to be something of a—free spirit, wants to be unfettered by the law—that sort of thing."

"There are fetters," said the inspector darkly, "and then there are fetters. He'd best go carefully, or he may get a taste of the real thing. But go on."

"That really is all, I think, Inspector. I'm sorry if it turns out to be nothing, but I thought someone should know. I'm really concerned about Barbara Dean."

"I'll see to it that someone lets you know as soon as we learn anything, Mrs. Martin, and thank you."

I fell into a troubled nap that afternoon, full of the kind of dream you'd rather not remember when you wake. This time I was driving my car down a steep hill into the river, over and over, jerking partly awake just as the water threatened to close over my face, and then starting the whole terrifying sequence over again. It was a relief when the phone by the bed roused me.

"Mrs. Martin? Morrison here. I've only negative news, I'm afraid, but I thought you'd want to know. We searched Mrs. Dean's house—a neighbor had a key—and there's no sign of her, nor clue to her whereabouts. Her handbag is gone, but her clothing and luggage seem to be in place, so far as we can tell. There's no convenient telephone number scribbled on a pad, no lovely railway guide left open to a particular page—nothing. It seems she simply left on a normal errand—though how, with her car in the garage?—and didn't return. We're trying to trace her earlier movements, where her car was seen, that sort of thing."

I absorbed that for a moment. "You might check with Mrs. Williamson at the bookshop," I offered. "I didn't see her speak to Barbara when she left so abruptly yesterday, but I suppose they might have talked earlier in the morning about Barbara's plans for the rest of the day." Actually, I doubted it; Barbara wasn't the type to confide in anyone else. But I was trying desperately to be useful.

"That's certainly a possibility," said the inspector politely. He didn't think much of the idea, either. "At any rate, it's a place to start. We'll be in touch."

So much for being useful. I went downstairs in search of friendly, purry company, but the cats led me straight to the door and stood there expectantly, tails erect. The mist had cleared.

I let them out, wandered miserably into my parlor, and sank down on the couch, wishing my own fog would clear. I felt dragged out and depressed, and my headache had returned. I couldn't seem to think. My mind was stuck on a treadmill, repeating itself over and over, like my dream.

Where was Barbara Dean? Her car was in the garage, where was she? She'd gone out and not come back, where was she? If she'd left town, she would have packed a bag. She would have canceled her engagements. She would have told someone. And if she hadn't left town, WHERE WAS SHE?

I presume I fed the cats and myself and read or something until it was time to go to bed. I know I tossed and turned for hours, finally falling into a fitful doze shortly before dawn, only to be jolted out of it by the phone. I picked it up, my blood racing fast enough to make my aching head much worse.

"Yes?"

"Mrs. Martin, Morrison here. I do apologize for ringing you so early, but I've been on the blower with the chief in London, and he was sure you'd want to know. He said to tell you he'd try to phone later." He cleared his throat, sounding as weary as I felt. "I'm afraid it's bad news. We've found Mrs. Dean."

I lay silent. His words could mean only one thing.

"Where?" I said at last.

"In the river. She'd been there for at least twenty-four hours, but she didn't drown—no water in the lungs. I'm afraid it's unquestionably murder."

17

"I SEE." It was no surprise, but the confirmation was still a terrible shock. I'd hoped I was wrong. There were so many questions, but I was numb. The inspector cleared his throat.

"The chief asked me to stress what I would have said in any case. You must be very careful, Mrs. Martin. Not all the connections between this murder and the Town Hall case are yet apparent, but it seems evident that they exist. We think, and this is conjecture at this point, and confidential, that Mrs. Dean was killed because she knew something in connection with the Town Hall murder. Our villain could very well decide you know too much, as well."

"I don't know anything," I said bitterly.

"You inferred a connection between Mrs. Dean and an old scandal. And now Mrs. Dean is dead. If the murderer thinks you know more than you do . . . well, the chief specifically said I was not to forbid you to look into matters, but he and I would both appreciate your—er—discretion. To be quite candid, I don't need any more on my plate at the moment, especially not the murder of my chief's—er—"

My mind was sluggishly coming to life. "Why the river? I mean, why did you look there?"

There was the faint hint of a sigh on the line. "The last place we were able to trace Mrs. Dean's car to was a car park hard by Lanterngate bridge. There is an attendant who patrols several car parks to make sure the cars are displaying the slips that show they've paid. Hers was the only car there shortly after five, and it was gone—in fact, the car park was empty—the next time the attendant came round, about seven. We don't know when it arrived back at her garage, or who drove it there. Except that it was quite evidently not Mrs. Dean."

"Evidently. Look, Inspector, there's a lot more I want to know, but you sound dead on your feet. I'll call you later. And please don't worry about me. I promise I'll look after myself."

In fact all I wanted to do was turn over and sleep and sleep. But even in the face of sudden death, cats want to be fed. I went about the chore mechanically, and of course they noticed. My cats are very fond of their housekeeper/cook, and when something is wrong with me, they know. I dragged back up to bed after they'd had their breakfast, and they trotted right after me, Emmy settling on my chest and Sam on my feet, and purred themselves to sleep. Their presence was so comforting I actually slept myself, and for nearly two hours enjoyed the blessing of dreamless oblivion.

When I woke for good I was in fighting trim—rested, angry, and ready to do battle.

And the first battle was with the Pettifers.

It was time Clarice answered some questions, and Archie as well. I was through with fencing. Barbara Dean was dead. I'd wished ever since I met her that I could really get to know that cool, detached woman. I admired her executive ability and agreed with her about many things, and lately she'd unbent enough to let me hope that someday we could become friends.

Now that could never happen. Someone had taken the

chance away from us, and I couldn't help blaming myself. If I had just been quicker on the uptake, I might have learned what Barbara knew, and the two of us . . .

The two of you might have been killed together, said a voice in my head that sounded remarkably like Alan's.

Well, at any rate, what was past was past and I couldn't undo it, but I could take some action now. I heaved myself out of bed and headed for the shower.

Bob Finch was hard at work when I was ready to leave.

"I suppose you've heard about Mrs. Dean?" I called out the back door.

"Wot abaht 'er?"

"Oh, dear." I went out and lowered my voice. "I thought you would have heard, or I wouldn't have brought it up. She's dead. She was found in the river, murdered."

It takes a lot to shock a Cockney. Bob processed the information stolidly as he plied his spade.

"Pore lady," he said finally. "Nice enough, under all 'er lah-di-dah ways. I 'ope as 'ow Mr. Archibald Bleedin' Pettifer 'as 'imself a better alibi for this one than 'ee 'as for the first."

"Bob!" I raised my voice, and he looked up at me in mild surprise. "Sorry, I didn't mean to shout. But what do you know about Mr. Pettifer's alibi for the first murder?"

" 'Ee 'asn't got one, that's wot." He resumed his digging. "I never said nothin', not wantin' to get a man in trouble. But if 'ee's done for a lady . . . madam, 'ee was never with that Benson, that night. I was in the King's 'Ead the 'ole time, and Benson, 'ee were drinkin' by 'isself."

My heart was beating very uncomfortably, but I had to be sure. "But Bob, if you were drinking yourself, were you—I mean, could you—"

"I weren't pissed," he said with dignity. "Not that night. Just mellowlike. An' I saw Benson come in, just after me, an' I saw 'im go up to 'is room abaht nine-thirty, lookin' like 'ee weren't feelin' so good. An' 'ee come back down in 'arf an hour an' drank 'isself silly. Wine, 'ee were drinkin'. 'Ee were still at it come closin' time, 'im bein' a resident in the pub and not 'avin' to observe licensin' hours. An' 'ee were alone the 'ole evenin'."

He turned his back decisively and I went back into the kitchen, stunned.

That seemed to settle it. Pettifer had no alibi, and had been lying about it. I hadn't been eager to believe Benson, but I trusted Bob.

I stalked to the garage for my car.

I'd forgotten how early it still was. Archie answered the door in his pajamas and bathrobe, red-faced and plainly furious. "And may I ask to what I owe this intrusion? Is a man to have no peace in his own home?" He stood in the doorway, his hand on the door, ready to slam it in my face.

"I must come in, Mr. Pettifer. You don't want to discuss this on your doorstep."

"I've nothing whatever to discuss with you, Mrs. Martin, whether on my doorstep or elsewhere."

"I see." I was as angry as he. "I suppose you'd rather I went to the police to talk about where you were the night Jack Jenkins was murdered."

He took a step backwards and his face paled. "I was at the King's Head. The police know that."

"No, you weren't. May I come in, or do you really want to have this conversation in front of your neighbors?"

He might have bluffed it out, even then, but a weak, frightened voice came from the stairway. "What is it, Archie? What's the matter? Who are you shouting at?"

Archie raised his hands in exasperation and turned his back, leaving me to walk in and close the door behind me. Clarice, clutching a filmy peignoir with one hand and the stair rail with the other, did not look glad to see me.

I would have preferred to talk to Archie alone, but there was no backing out now. "I'm sorry, but I think we'd better sit down, all three of us. Are you all right, Clarice? Do you need help?" The shadows under her eyes looked like bruises, and her skin and hair were dull and not very clean. She looked very ill indeed, but she shrank away from my touch and clung to Archie, who deposited her on an overstuffed white sofa in the front room and stood guard over her.

"Very well, Mrs. Martin. You've succeeded in invading our home and frightening my wife. Now state your business and go."

Clarice made a little squeak, of nerves or protest.

"It isn't quite that simple," I said, sitting without invitation in the nearest chair. "I need some answers, and I intend to get them or turn the questions over to the police. You see, I've been talking to Bob Finch. I believe him to be a reliable witness, at least as long as he's sober, which he says he was, more or less, on the Sunday night when Jack Jenkins was killed."

Clarice sobbed and buried her head against Archie's chest; he reached a protective arm around her but never moved his gaze from my face.

"He says, Mr. Pettifer, that Herbert Benson was drinking alone all that evening, except for a little time when he went up to his room. He says you were never with him, nor was anyone else.

"Now that, of course, was presumably the time Jenkins was killed. And if—" I faltered, looking at Clarice, but I had to go on with it. "If what I've heard is true, that you—knew Jack very well—you might have had reason to kill him. I've told the police some of this, but not all of it, not what Bob said. I thought it would be only fair to see if you had some explanation before I went to them."

Archie sat down heavily next to Clarice and put his head in his hands. Clarice sobbed quietly. The only other sound in the room was the ticking of the clock.

"Yes," he finally said, raising his head and taking one of

Clarice's hands firmly in his. His bluster was gone, replaced by a kind of desperate dignity. "Yes, you're quite right. I'm sorry this had to come up in front of you, my dear," he said to Clarice, "but the truth is, I killed Jack. He was my son, you see. There was a barmaid, years ago—at any rate, he'd come to town to make a scandal just when the Town Hall deal was at a critical point. I'd paid support for him, all the years when he was growing up and turning into a young lout, and worse. But now that wasn't enough; he wanted more. He planned to tell lies about how badly I'd treated him unless I paid him a great deal of money.

"I didn't intend to kill him. I went to the Town Hall after the Lord Mayor's meeting; we'd agreed on that spot as private. He—he taunted me and I pushed him, and—"

He couldn't go on. He shook his head and made a repudiating, pushing-away movement of his hands, and then turned to gather Clarice into his arms, but she struggled free.

"No." Tears were streaming down her face, but she struggled to control her sobs. "No, I won't let you. It was me, Dorothy. It was me, all the time."

"My dear—"

"*No*, Archie, I have to tell it. Don't look at me like that. Go away, over there—" she pointed to the other side of the room "—and don't look at me at all. Then maybe I can say it."

She drew a shuddering breath, gathered herself together with a kind of threadbare courage, and fixed her eyes on me. "I thought Archie was meeting a woman, you see. He'd been so—odd, lately. Angry, and wouldn't talk to me. I know now he was worried about—that boy—but I thought—anyway, I decided they'd meet at the Town Hall after Archie had finished with his dinner meeting, and I went there to wait for them. You do see, don't you?"

Archie started to speak, but I turned so fierce a glare on him that he stopped and looked away.

"I went to the side door, of course. I was sure I was too early—I knew the meeting would go on for hours and it was only about nine—but after a bit, when nothing happened, I began to think they were already inside, and I couldn't bear it. So I tried the door and it was unlocked. I crept inside, trying not to make any noise, and he nearly frightened me to death."

"Archie?"

"No—that—that boy. It wasn't dark outside yet, of course, but it was like midnight in that back hall. And he laughed, out of the darkness, and then switched a torch on my face. I was blinded, and so frightened, but he only laughed some more. And then he switched the torch off, and he said, 'So this must be the little wifey. Well, well. Let's go someplace where we can get to know each other.' And he grabbed my arm—I nearly screamed, then, but my throat was all closed up and I couldn't—and he held the torch to the floor and pulled me through the front of the building to some frightful sort of cupboard and shut the door and turned on the light."

"And told you who he was?"

"Yes, presently, but he didn't have to. I knew. He looked so like Archie when he was younger. Of course, Archie never dressed like that—he cares about his appearance, and he's always clean. But—oh, I can't explain, the eyes, the cheekbones—I knew.

"And then he started saying how much he needed money, and how upset Archie would be if he thought I knew about him, and perhaps we could work something out—oh, I can't remember everything he said, because I was so frightened, and I kept thinking about the son I'd always wanted to have and never could, and here was this—this—hooligan claiming to be

Archie's son, and I didn't want it to be true, but I knew it was. And I tried to get away, but he ran after me out into the hallway and grabbed my arm, and I turned around and pushed as hard as I could—but we were standing next to the stairs, and he fell, and—and then he just lay there, so still, on the landing, and I thought I heard something, and I turned and ran, and ran . . ."

She took out a handkerchief and blew her nose.

I cleared my throat. "Clarice, dear, don't you think you'd better—"

"No. I have to finish it. I went home and waited for hours, but when Archie finally came home I couldn't talk to him after all. I pretended to be asleep. I thought we could talk later, when I wasn't so upset. I—I didn't know the boy was dead, you see. And then when you found the body, I nearly lost my mind, but I realized they might blame Archie, and I would have to be clever. If I just kept on saying nothing about it, with a bit of luck no one would connect the dead boy with us. And when things seemed to calm down, I thought it would be all right. But you wouldn't leave it alone."

"I couldn't—I didn't know—"

"It wasn't your fault. It wasn't anybody's fault. And I think I'm glad you know, now. I couldn't let Archie take the blame for what I did. I'm tired, Archie."

She looked up at him and he strode across the room to her, and the doorbell rang.

I knew it would be Inspector Morrison even before I looked out the window and saw the police car. I walked to the door and opened it; Archie and Clarice were oblivious, lost in their own world of sorrow and grief.

"I think you'd better come in, Inspector." I had to clear my throat before I could go on. "There's been—Clarice has confessed to the murder. But give them a moment, if you can. They need to forgive each other before the law steps in."

18

T H E   M O R N I N G   W A S   nearly spent before I was able, very shakily, to drive home. I'd had to repeat everything I'd been told. Then Clarice had been asked to make her statement all over again, with a sergeant taking it down, and after she was taken away, Archie, still sitting limply on the beautiful, sterile white couch, had to explain his part in the confusing events of the evening.

"It was about ten when I finally left the meeting and went to the Town Hall to meet Jack. When I saw the side door standing wide open, I was angry; I'd given Jack the key against my better judgment and told him to keep the door shut and locked until I got there. I went in intending to give him a piece of my mind, but I couldn't find him. I didn't dare call out very loudly or switch on a light; it wasn't yet really dark outside and there were still people on the streets. I stumbled about and finally risked the light in the broom cupboard."

"And he was in there, I suppose," said the inspector. "Head injuries affect people oddly; they can sometimes walk about for a bit before they collapse."

"No, he wasn't there. The room was empty. I left the light

on with the door almost shut, and it gave me enough light to see—on the landing—"

He couldn't go on for a moment, and the inspector waited patiently enough.

Archie blew his nose and continued. "He was my son, Inspector. I'd never known him very well, and he was no good, and he was making my life a misery to me, but he was my only son, and he was dead. Inspector, when can I see my wife?"

"Presently, sir. Go on with your story."

Gray and weary, Archie pulled himself together with visible effort. "Where was I?"

"You'd just seen Jack, on the landing."

"Yes, well, it was a terrible shock. I went down to him, of course, but—well, it only took a moment to know that—that there was nothing I could do. And after a bit I started to think about my position. I ought to have called the police right then, but—you would have wanted to know why I was there, and the whole story would have come out. I thought, if I could move him—hide him until I could think what to do—I knew I shouldn't, but I wanted some time.

"So I carried him up the stairs, just half a flight to the ground floor, and put him in the cupboard. It would have been better to get him out of the Hall altogether, but with people about, and the twilight, I didn't dare. And it was—it was dreadful." He shuddered strongly. "He was still warm and limp; he couldn't have been dead very long. I thought I could deal with the nightmare better after I'd had some sleep. I did search his pockets as best I could in the dark, because I wanted to get my key back—I knew that would lead straight to me—but I couldn't find it.

"That was why I came back Monday morning, to find the key and take away any identification. I'd quite forgotten it was Mrs. Finch's day, and the sound of her scream put the wind up me so badly I very nearly turned tail and ran. But there was nothing for it but to bluff it out. I searched the body while she and Mrs. Martin were having their tea, but the key was gone. There was nothing in his pockets at all. Inspector, I really must be allowed to see my wife."

It was a feeble imitation of Archie's usual bluster, and it didn't impress the inspector at all.

"After you have completed your statement, Mr. Pettifer," he said grimly. "Now tell me, sir, just when did you strike Jenkins on the jaw?"

Archie looked at him without comprehension. "Strike him? I didn't strike him. I tried to be as careful as I could, moving him. It was almost—I couldn't help feeling I ought not to hurt him. Silly, I knew that—but I told you, he was my son."

"And why did you lie about where you were that night?"

"I—it was stupid. I don't know. I couldn't say where I really was, but that weak story—it was Benson's idea. He said he'd vouch for me, and no one could prove I wasn't there, and at the time it seemed reasonable. I—I'm almost glad it's all out— lately he's been hinting that he'd have to tell the truth, and I didn't know what to do—it's been hell." He dropped his head into his hands, but the inspector took no notice.

"And what can you tell us about Mrs. Dean?" he asked in the same level, implacable tone.

Archie just blinked, looking as if he couldn't quite remember who Mrs. Dean was. "What about Mrs. Dean? What does she have to do with any of it?" He brushed his hand across his eyes, but the tears welled up again. "Inspector, I implore you—"

His voice broke, and Morrison rose. "Very well, we'll talk again later. Sergeant Tanner will transcribe your statement for you to sign at the station. If you'll come with me, we'll see if you can be allowed to speak with Mrs. Pettifer for a few moments."

I had to turn away; it was indecent to look at the naked longing in Archie's face. Whatever had caused him to bully his wife, I thought, shaken, it hadn't been a lack of love. It was there, raw, powerful, frightening.

When I got home I wanted two things quite desperately, and couldn't get either of them. I needed to talk things out with Alan so badly it was a physical longing, and I needed a very large, very powerful drink. It's a bad idea to drink out of necessity, but there are exceptions to every rule.

Of course, Alan was still in London. Presumably. I called his office with no hope at all, and my pessimism was fully justified. "Very late this evening" was the best guess about his return. I left a message that he was to call, no matter how late, and sat considering my second problem.

I'd been meaning for some time to stock up on liquor, but I hadn't been planning a party, so there was no hurry. Now there was literally not a drop of anything alcoholic in the house, barring the vanilla. Jane wasn't home, apparently—there was no movement visible in the windows on the side of her house I could see from mine.

I was so tired I could barely move, but I couldn't nap. The thoughts in my head wouldn't cease their squirrel-cage chase.

Furthermore, I knew I needed to eat, even though I was too upset to be hungry, and I still hadn't bought groceries. And there was that dress I needed to return to Mrs. Hawkins at the King's Head. I got out the car.

My mind was working so badly, I was actually inside the door of the pub before I remembered that I might well run into Benson, and I nearly turned and left. But I could always snub him, I reasoned. And I truly needed something to eat, and yes, all right, at least a moderate something to drink.

Mrs. Hawkins, when she came bustling to greet me at the bar, reassured me. "Thank you, dearie, you didn't need to worry about the dress, but ta all the same. And you needn't think you may be bothered with Mr. Benson; he's away for the weekend, left early this morning. Now, it's a bit early for lunch, but can we do you a sandwich? There's cold ham and cold beef, or salmon if you'd like, or a salad, or a ploughman's, of course—"

"A cold beef sandwich would be lovely," I said hastily, before she could list the entire contents of her larder. "And do you stock bourbon whiskey?"

I was settled with a large bourbon—neat—and a huge, crusty sandwich with salad and pickles, in what seemed like a few seconds. I prudently ate some of the food first and then sipped the drink with appreciation. It tasted good, but I didn't want it as much as I'd thought. Mrs. Hawkins's conversation flowed over me soothingly, calming my troubled thoughts as she moved about the bar, polishing the beer handles, wiping the glasses.

"And you could've knocked me over with a feather when they told us, me and Derek." I realized she was talking, not about the Pettifers, but about the discovery of Barbara Dean's body, and tried to concentrate. Somehow it didn't seem as important as it had earlier. I couldn't stop thinking about meek little Clarice and bullying Archie, now cast in roles befitting neither of them.

". . . and just outside our door, too, would you believe it?"

She was waiting for me to answer a question. "I'm sorry, what? I was—distracted." I'd drunk more of the bourbon than I'd intended. I pushed the glass away.

"It's all right, dear, you look tired to death. I just said, who'd have thought it, a lovely lady like her, to jump in the river? Why would she go and do a thing like that?"

I wasn't going to debate the manner of Barbara's death with Mrs. Hawkins. "It's very sad," I said, shaking my head. "And that was lovely, but I'd better be getting home." I was taking no chances about Benson. "Oh, and could I buy a bottle of Jack Daniel's to take with me?"

"There, now, just you take this." She thrust a bottle into my hands. "We don't have an off-license, but you bring us a fresh bottle one day. You look as though you could do with the stuff now."

I went home and slept like a baby for most of the afternoon. Kindness was the real cure.

WITH WAKING, THOUGH, came memory, and with memory came pain. I went downstairs, fed the cats, and then walked restlessly in my garden, where Bob had made some impressive progress, though it was still a disaster area. Picking up a leaf or a twig here and there, I tried to wipe out the pictures that kept replaying across my mind. The look on Clarice's face as she talked about the son she'd never had—and on Archie's, talking about the son he did have, who died trying to blackmail him. It was no use. Nothing would ever erase those images from my memory.

There was the image, too, of Archie with his arms around his wife as she sobbed against him. Those two had begun to understand each other this morning.

Yes, and what good was that going to do them? England doesn't execute murderers anymore—and Clarice would probably be charged with something short of murder, in any case—but she'd be away for a very long time. And would Archie begin to brood about her killing his son, for whatever reason, however accidentally? Would he end by hating her—or she him, for giving another woman the child she wanted?

The bells from the cathedral tower had been sounding over my head for quite a while, I suddenly realized. Evensong was about to begin. I didn't even bother to wash my hands or tidy my hair, just walked straight across the Close and slipped into an obscure place as the choir was beginning the first psalm. Here, at least, was peace and respite.

And in the calm and quiet of the great cathedral, with time-less chant washing over me and light from the altar candles gently touching the incomparable beauty of carved stone and wood, my mind slowed and hushed and began to work properly again. Through the familiar words, one layer of my mind replayed the morning's scene yet once again, but analytically this time.

And I realized I didn't believe it.

Very well, why not? They weren't lying. No one lies that convincingly. They both meant every word they said. Well, at least Archie was lying at first, but that was to protect Clarice. He must have guessed the truth by then. But later, in his statement to the police, he was telling the truth.

Yes, that felt right. And Clarice's statement, tearful, wrenched out of her by her fear for Archie—she was telling the truth, too, surely. I knelt for the General Confession, and its words intertwined with mental protests: . . . *the devices and desires of our own hearts. We have left undone those things which we ought to have done.* . . . Yes, there's too much left unanswered. How did Jack's jaw get broken? Clarice couldn't possibly have done it, and Archie claimed he'd never touched him, except to drag him upstairs. And he was telling the truth. And what happened to the key?

The rest of the prayers droned on, unheard, as I considered other questions. Who killed Barbara Dean, and why? It certainly wasn't Clarice. Archie hadn't even seemed to know she was dead. And what was the Sheffield connection? I was sure there was one, but had the police looked into the matter of one George Crenshawe?

It was an anonymous-sounding name. Of course! I made some small noise that I had to turn into a cough to reassure the woman kneeling next to me. Why hadn't I realized until now that the man could be operating under another name? Nothing was easier. Assume that the Sheffield investigation had uncovered criminal culpability in the building of those council flats. George Crenshawe was long gone by that time. Why shouldn't he be here, in Sherebury as—well, why not as a nasty-tempered builder named Farrell?

I surfaced for the benediction, and accepted it gratefully, but as I walked home through the brilliant sunshine of a July evening my mind was wholly occupied with my new theory. I thought about it as I made myself supper of toast and tea, with a little whiskey thrown in. I thought about it as I curled up on the couch with two contented cats.

I was still thinking about it when the doorbell rang, a little after eleven. I sat up in alarm, and the cats scattered. What new, terrible thing, at this hour—?

"Dorothy, it's me."

The voice came through the open window, deep and low. I was at the door in two seconds, and in Alan's arms, crying in sheer relief.

Bless the man, he let me cry, holding me and making soothing, meaningless noises. And when I'd slowed down a little, he handed me a box of tissues and sat me down on the couch, and disappeared into the kitchen. The marvelous smell of coffee floated into the parlor. When Alan came back, he was carrying a tray with steaming cups and a large plate of cookies.

"Where on earth did you find those?" I said with a last, shaky sniffle. "I would have sworn the cupboard was as bare as Mother Hubbard's."

"Fortnum's best biscuits. I bought them as a peace offering." He put the tray on the coffee table and sat down beside me. "Just as well I did. You need some sugar, woman. Eat."

I ate, and drank. Alan makes marvelous coffee, much better than mine, and the cookies were rich and delicious.

"I'm sorry I made such a fool of myself," I said finally.

"Not to worry. You've had rather a trying day."

That made me giggle, as perhaps he had intended. Talk about the English gift for understatement! But I sobered quickly. He'd obviously talked to Morrison.

"Alan, it isn't true. I'm sure it isn't, but I'm not sure what's wrong with it. They're both telling the truth, but there are too many things that don't fit."

He nodded. "I've had a quick briefing from Morrison, and he agrees. We've had to charge Clarice, of course; she's confessed to manslaughter. But—" He spread his hands wearily. "She'll be out on bail tomorrow, I expect."

"Oh, Alan, that's wonderful! I'd forgotten about bail. I was picturing her—" I had to reach for the tissues again, but I mopped up hastily. "No, I'm all right. I'm not going to come apart on you again. Alan, I'm so glad you're here."

"I must leave soon. Tomorrow is a frantic day, and, of course, Sunday will be even worse. Then it'll be over."

"Over? How can you be so sure—oh, yes, the royal visit. I'd forgotten."

He gave a great guffaw. "Here I've been working myself to a shadow over nothing else, and you've forgotten that the Prince of Wales is coming to town."

"Well, I hadn't actually forgotten. I mean, that's why you've been away so much. But compared to what happened this morning, it just didn't seem very important, somehow, and it slipped my mind. I'm so worried about the Pettifers, Alan."

He put his arm around my shoulders and hugged me close. "You have a greater capacity for worrying about people you don't even care for than anyone else I know. I think that's one reason I love you so much."

He turned my face toward his, and this time the kiss was not on the cheek. It went on a long time, and when he stood up to leave, we were both a little shaky.

"Good night, my dear. Get some sleep. I'll ring you tomorrow."

19

ONE OF LIFE'S great blessings is that death and tragedy are never allowed to take full possession. Life goes on. People say it bitterly, as if one ought to be occupied solely with the current disaster. In fact we couldn't cope if, in the midst of crisis, people didn't eat and drink and relax a bit and comfort one another.

Alan had comforted me. I slept very late the next morning, waking only at the insistence of the cats (who also make sure I take a balanced view of life's problems—their needs coming high on the list). After coffee I felt ready to deal rationally with serious problems. What was left of Saturday morning was spent waiting for Alan to call, and making lists of what I knew (or felt I could safely conjecture), and what I wanted to know.

KNOWN

1. Jack Jenkins was blackmailing Archie, and tried to blackmail Clarice.

2. If he recognized George Crenshawe under some other name in Sherebury, Jack would probably have tried to blackmail him, too.

3. Barbara Dean might also have recognized Crenshawe.
4. Jack's jaw was broken. Not by Clarice or Archie.
5. Somebody took Archie's key from Jack, or from his body.

NEED TO KNOW

1. Where's the key?
2. Who hit Jack hard enough to break his jaw, and when?
3. Is Crenshawe in Sherebury, and if so, WHO IS HE?
4. Who killed Barbara?

A meager harvest, but concentrating on the puzzle kept me from thinking, over and over, about yesterday's horrors. I studied the piece of paper and then added a sixth point to the first list.

6. Crenshawe is bald in the newspaper picture.

The point that interested me the most, of course, was the identity of Crenshawe. If I was right, he was at the center of these crimes, which would seem to take Mavis Underwood, the Lord Mayor, and John Thorpe right out of the picture. None of them, by the remotest stretch of the imagination, could be Crenshawe. Only Farrell seemed to fit the bill, and he was emphatically not bald.

But the others could have some connection with Crenshawe.

My mind had just dredged up that unhelpful suggestion when the phone rang.

"Morning, love. I have exactly five minutes before I must meet the Prince's advance guard."

"I thought he didn't get to town until tomorrow."

"Nor does he. His people arrive today. Now don't interrupt; there isn't time. I called, first, to tell you that Clarice is home, still insisting she's a killer. Second, how are you holding up?"

I hadn't thought about it. "I'm fine. How's Clarice feeling?"

"Bloody, I gather from Morrison. Look, my time is fully occupied until about nine tomorrow evening, when we thankfully pack His Royal Highness back to Kensington Palace. I can't go to the concert with you—I've got to do the official—but after the reception is over and he's gone, we're going on a carouse, just the two of us, and I shall brook no interference. Understood?"

"Yes, sir," I said demurely. "Orders received and understood, sir."

He chuckled. "Carry on, Lieutenant!" He pronounced it "leftenant," and I saluted smartly as I hung up the phone.

Amazing how a few words on the phone could make the sky brighter, the air sweeter. I thought I'd outgrown that sort of thing years ago.

How nice that I hadn't!

Abandoning for the moment my unproductive speculations, I ate a few of Alan's biscuits as a stand-in for lunch and decided to go to the bookshop. Although I dreaded questions about the Pettifers, work was good therapy. Perhaps it would jump-start my stalled mind.

Fortunately, the cathedral grapevine had been operating at full roar, with the result that every detail of the Pettifer drama was already known by the time I showed up. Willie, bless her heart, had the sense to see I didn't want to talk about it, and the two rather scared new volunteers who were trying to take the place of Barbara and Clarice treated me like a leper. I wanted to tell them tragedy wasn't catching, but after all, I was just as pleased to be left alone to do my job.

The work did keep my mind from dwelling on the two women who should have been there, but by late afternoon I still hadn't made any mental connections that would help Clarice. This one, I thought grimly, is going to take a miracle.

One was waiting in the wings.

I volunteered to straighten up the shop after closing time.

The others had worked all day, and were eager to get home; with Alan occupied, I had nothing to do for the evening but go to the supermarket, a chore I can put off indefinitely. And I felt I wanted to be alone there, anyway. Perhaps, with half the shop lights out and no one else around, I'd have the chance to tell Barbara Dean I was sorry.

A person gets odd notions in a medieval cathedral.

Or maybe not so odd, after all. For as I worked my way down the shelves, tidying, I found myself drawn to the poetry section, where no work needed to be done. And I'll swear to my dying day that it was Barbara Dean who made me take that volume of George Herbert from the shelf again and stare at it.

The cover design was rather ornate, suitable for a poet who died in 1633. A little typographical ornament separated the words George and Herbert, and as I looked at it in the half-light, slightly out of focus, it transformed itself into an equals sign.

George = Herbert.

George Crenshawe equals Herbert Benson.

That was what Barbara had seen. It was all so obvious once I saw it myself that I sagged, openmouthed, against the book-shelves. That bright-brown hair—not a dye job, a wig. And all those rings would have made a perfectly acceptable substitute for brass knuckles. And—I slapped myself on the forehead—surely he was from Sheffield! He'd as much as said so: "Archie and I are good friends, old friends."

Now that, I thought, was an exaggeration. He was a good deal younger than Archie. He probably knew him slightly, being in the same trade. But it certainly seemed to put him in Sheffield many years ago, when Archie lived there. So why not three years ago, when a building burned down?

But wait a minute. Bob Finch had said Benson had been drinking alone all that Sunday night, when Jack was killed. I stood up straight and walked back to the staff room. Forget tidying up, I needed to sit and think about this.

He hadn't said quite that, had he? I collapsed in the armchair and played back Bob's words. He'd said Benson had come in a little after he, Bob, had. And then he was drinking alone until—until—yes! Until he went up to his room for half an hour!

How did Bob know where Benson went when he left the bar? Even if he saw him start up the stairs—and you could see the main stairs from one corner of the bar—there were back stairs.

Now, exactly what might have happened? Suppose Jack had recognized Benson/Crenshawe, maybe a day or two before, and decided to try another spot of blackmail while he was at it. Very well. He already had an appointment with his father in the Town Hall, and he'd wangled the key out of him. He could have made an earlier appointment with Benson.

All right. So Sunday night comes. Clarice—oh, yes, this was working out perfectly! Clarice goes to spy on Archie and finds Jack instead. He upsets her so much she pushes him down the stairs and runs away, terrified because she hears a noise!

And that noise is Benson. He's sneaked away from the King's Head to keep his appointment. He must have already had some idea of murder in his mind, or he wouldn't have been so careful to cover his tracks. Anyway, he finds Clarice there and hides until she leaves, and then sees Jack, who's staggered up the stairs, just beginning to recover. It's too good an opportunity to waste. He pastes him one on the jaw hard enough to break the jawbone, hard enough to crush Jack's head against the cruel carved oak. He satisfies himself that Jack is dead, takes everything out of his pockets, and is about to get out of there, locking the door behind him with the key he found, when the third of Jack's victims enters the scene. Benson sneaks out through the open door, leaving Archie to his terrible discovery, and goes back to the pub, where he checks to make sure there's no blood on his clothes and "comes back down from his room." And drinks enough to float a battleship, according to Bob.

The very thought made my mouth dry, and I got up to make

a pot of tea. That all seemed to make sense, I thought as I sank into the chair again, the tray beside me on the rickety table. Benson could drink quite a lot, as I was in a position to know. He'd drunk himself nearly blotto the night I'd been forced to have dinner with him.

The night—oh, dear God! I spilled my tea before I carefully released the cup from my suddenly shaking hand.

He'd been drinking hard that night for the same reason he'd been drinking hard the night Bob saw him. He'd just committed murder. While we were sitting at the table, Barbara Dean was floating in the river a few yards away. I had dined with a murderer, his victim barely cold.

I made it to the sink before I was sick.

I cleaned up the mess myself, too. Fortunately I'd eaten very little all day. My mind kept repeating that phrase: Fortunately I've eaten very little . . . I went into the kind of autopilot that serves us so well in shock, doing what needs to be done, thinking of trivial practicalities. Let's see, I'd better shut up the shop properly and then have someone walk me home, I'm pretty shaky.

After I'd carefully checked the till—empty—and the tea-kettle and lights—off—one of the vergers was happy to see me to my door. They were all working frantically to cope with to-night's festival concert, and then get the cathedral brushed and polished for the Prince, who was to attend the concert tomorrow night, after he'd dedicated the hospital. My man was ready for a little break, but very excited about the royal visit; he talked nonstop for the short walk across the Close to my house. I responded politely and thanked him at my door, and then walked the few more steps to Jane's house.

"No, I won't come in, thanks. I'm not feeling very well. I think reaction's set in, from yesterday. But I need to eat something, and I've absolutely no food in the house. Could I borrow some bread and eggs, or maybe something frozen? No, really, it's very kind of you, but I'd rather be alone."

I didn't dare be with Jane. I'd talk if I were with Jane, and the coldly rational part of my brain, the only part functioning, told me silence was much safer.

For there was absolutely nothing I could do with my new information. Indeed, it wasn't information at all, but guesswork. I refused to go over it all again, but I knew there wasn't one single verifiable piece of evidence in the whole scenario. Everything needed to be checked, confirmed, nailed down by the police before there was any kind of case.

And every senior policeman who could deal properly with it was occupied for the next twenty-seven hours with His Royal Highness, the Prince of Wales.

I'll never know how I managed to stay inside my skin for those next few hours. I ate something Jane supplied, without tasting it, and then sat with a book in my lap and the TV turned on, paying attention to neither, until it was time to go to bed.

That was possibly the worst part. I'd never been afraid of the dark, and after sleeping alone for over a year, I'd gotten over jumpiness. Now, every slight creak of the old house, every tap of tree branch against window, brought me wide awake, muscles tense, heart pounding. About two o'clock, I began to wonder whether I had really locked all the doors and windows downstairs. I was afraid to get up and check, and afraid not to. I finally tiptoed downstairs in the dark and checked everything—locked, of course—and scurried back up to bed with my heart beating so painfully fast I lay and worried about having a heart attack. I'd just made myself relax a little when I heard footsteps on the stairs.

I very nearly *did* have a heart attack before I realized the intruder was Emmy.

That did it; enough was enough. I rummaged in my medicine cabinet and found two antihistamine tablets, which always knock me out. I woke only when church bells roused me, dry-mouthed from the cold tablets but in my right mind.

I was in no danger. I never had been. Benson—it was easier to go on thinking of him as Benson—had no idea I suspected anything. And this was Sunday, a beautiful summer Sunday in the most civilized, law-abiding country on earth. As long as I acted normal, pursued my usual activities and kept my mouth shut, I would come to no harm. And in a few hours—I glanced at my watch—in thirteen hours or so, I could turn the whole terrible business over to Alan and retire from the field.

The amateur sleuths who got into trouble, I reminded myself, were the ones who went off on their own, performing silly heroics. Obviously, an intelligent person who minded her own business was perfectly safe.

I had reckoned without the influence of the Church.

Since I would normally attend Matins and the Eucharist on a Sunday morning, I fed the cats, got dressed, and made my way across the Close. I did try to be a little late, so I wouldn't have to talk to anyone. Then I would leave early, for the same reason, stick close to home until time for the concert, and tell Alan my whole story as soon as I possibly could.

All went according to plan until we got to the psalm appointed for the day. I was enjoying the harmonies of the male choir until the words began to get through to me. ". . . It is God that girdeth me with strength . . . He teacheth mine hands to fight . . . I will follow upon mine enemies and overtake them; neither will I turn again till I have destroyed them. . . ."

The rest of the lessons were a call to action, as well, the sermon followed suit, and to top it off, the final hymn was "Onward, Christian Soldiers!"

Now, I'm not the superstitious type. I don't try to solve problems by opening the Bible at random and reading a verse, and I think it's downright presumptuous to go around asking for a sign from above.

On the other hand, when I'm bombarded with messages all saying the same thing, I do begin to wonder.

Jane caught up with me as I hurried home. "No coffee this morning, Dorothy?" She was panting; my legs are longer than hers.

"Not this morning," I said, smiling but not slacking my pace. "I'll talk to you later; there's something I have to do."

If only I were sure what!

There was no point in pretending, I thought to myself over coffee in the kitchen, that I was fired solely by zeal to do what might possibly be my Christian duty. The truth was, inaction had never suited me. Common sense be damned; I wanted to charge off in some direction or other. My problem, as usual, was to decide which direction.

Very well. I dug in a drawer for my lists and consulted them. They were no help at all. I now knew the answers to all my questions. The trouble was proving the story, and that was police work.

Yes, but was it?

The police couldn't take action for several hours yet, and meanwhile, what was Benson up to? Mrs. Hawkins had said he was away for the weekend. What if he was escaping at this very moment? What if someone else knew too much, and he was busy disposing of another body? What if . . . ?

What if I could uncover some proof of Benson's guilt while he was away? That would force the police, busy as they were, to take action—to find him, arrest him.

But where to look? He would have thrown the key to the Town Hall in the river long ago, surely. And the Hall itself could hold no clue; the police had searched it thoroughly, and they simply don't miss anything these days, even the most microscopic evidence.

But they hadn't, so far as I knew, searched Benson's room at the King's Head. Why would they? They had no reason to suspect him.

But I had.

20

THERE'S VIRTUALLY NO traffic in Sherebury on a Sunday morning, so I drove to the King's Head unscathed, parked my car, and went in to find Mrs. Hawkins busy setting tables for the lunchtime rush that would arrive in about an hour. I was the only customer in the place, and she served me my coffee with a preoccupied smile and immediately went back to her work. Good.

I paid my bill and drank two cups of excellent coffee as fast as I could, to provide myself with an excuse to go upstairs to the ladies' loo. I needn't have bothered; no one was paying the slightest attention.

After a genuinely necessary stop at the facilities, I turned the other way, toward the guest rooms. I didn't know which one was Benson's, of course, but for a long-term guest it would probably be one of the biggest and best the house had to offer. And in an old inn like this, that would mean a center room, looking out over either the river or the garden. With a guilty glance over my shoulder, I chose a likely door, knocked twice, and then took out my Swiss Army knife.

I've been teased about my extra-large, all-inclusive Swiss

Army knife, lying heavily at the bottom of my purse at all times. The fact remains that nothing comes in quite so handy in quite so many situations. I had even used mine for a spot or two of burglary before, but in every case on doors for which I possessed a legitimate key, somewhere. This door, loose-fitting, with an old lock, would have been easy if my hands hadn't been shaking and slippery with sweat. I dropped the knife with a clatter that sounded like the entire percussion section of a brass band—but no one came, and I doggedly carried on until the bolt slipped back and I was in.

It was a pleasant room with a little balcony. More to the point, it was the right one. I could see that at a glance. Even if I hadn't recognized the sport coat hanging over the back of a chair, the room bore signs of long occupancy—a half-empty box of cigars, a pile of well-thumbed magazines, no luggage in sight.

Very well. I was here. Now what?

It would have been easier if I'd known what I was looking for, but I was determined to be as thorough as possible, under the circumstances. I knew Alan would have my head if I disturbed evidence for the police, but I could look, so long as I was careful. I locked the door behind me and began.

A search of the clothes hanging in the wardrobe revealed nothing. Nothing in the pockets except what one would expect—train tickets, dirty handkerchiefs, shreds of tobacco. No stains I could see on any article of clothing.

The drawers were no more helpful. Besides the usual underwear and socks there was only a pornographic novel, lying offensively in the bedside drawer on top of the Gideon Bible. It was certainly nasty, but probably not illegal, and if there was anything hidden in it, I wasn't going to find it. I couldn't bring myself to pick the thing up, even with a tissue over my hand.

It was as I was about to check the bathroom that I heard footsteps. The wide old floorboards creaked as the steps drew nearer, and for a moment I couldn't think at all. The balcony?

Too small, no place to hide. The bathroom? I'd be discovered at once. In total panic I dropped to the floor and rolled under the bed.

Of course the steps went on past. "The wicked flee when no man pursueth." I lay and listened while whoever it was stopped at the end of the hall and a door opened and closed. My heart was pounding so loudly in my ears I had trouble hearing further movement, but when a toilet flushed, I was pretty sure I had heard a resident of the hotel, not an employee who might enter other rooms in turn. I could get up.

Sure, I could. Getting into that tight space with adrenaline pushing me all the way had been one thing. Forcing arthritic joints to get me out was another. I wiggled and grunted, and finally hooked my fingers into the bedsprings to give me some leverage.

But my left hand couldn't find a purchase. There was something in the way—not a bed slat, but something smooth that, as my fingers poked blindly at it, gave way and dropped onto my stomach.

Fingers and toes shoving against the springs, I managed finally to wriggle out from under, sit up, and look at my find.

It was a wallet, or at least a small black leather folder intended to carry papers of some sort. It bulged slightly in the middle.

It held two things. One was a ring, a heavily carved man's ring with small gold prongs bent slightly back where the stone had been.

The other was a key.

I managed to stand up, every joint protesting, and then sneezed six times in a row. The standard of housekeeping was very high at the King's Head, but even they did not dust the underside of the bedsprings very often.

Which created a dilemma. I had done exactly what I had warned myself not to do—tampered with evidence. I held in my hands the missing key to the Town Hall, and one of the rings Benson had been wearing when he had delivered a deathblow to Jack Jenkins.

They should have been left exactly where they were, with the dust on the springs but not on the wallet showing that they hadn't been there very long. But there was no point in putting them back now, not with my fingerprints all over them. Besides, Benson might realize they'd been disturbed and throw them out.

Why on earth hadn't he disposed of them? The answer, I supposed, lay in the setting that was missing from the ring. He'd kept the key to search for the stone in the Town Hall, where it must have fallen when he hit Jack. Some hope—the police would have found it long ago.

And maybe he'd kept the ring, stupidly, because it was valuable and he didn't think anyone would notice.

Well, no one had. I'd even seen that he wore one ring that didn't fit, that fell off, and thought nothing about what it might be replacing. I'd heard nothing about any gem being found—

Wait a minute! The police hadn't found it! Alan would have told me. And if they hadn't found it, it wasn't there. They use a vacuum at crime scenes these days, with a very fine filter, and sift through absolutely everything.

They hadn't found it. Pettifer said he hadn't found anything. Benson hadn't found it or he wouldn't have kept the key. That meant—

Mrs. Finch.

Dear Mrs. Finch, going around with her rags and her polish and her mop the next morning, scrubbing conscientiously in all the corners. Picking up something small and shiny, perhaps, and dropping it in her capacious handbag—and forgetting all about it when she discovered the body.

How long was it going to take Benson to make that same connection?

I peeked out the door before scuttling down the back stairs

and out the back door. I hadn't been able to lock Benson's door behind me, but that was the least of my worries just now.

Bob was still setting out wallflowers in my flower beds.

"Is your mother busy this afternoon, Bob?" I would have her over for tea, and casually bring up odd things I had found while cleaning, and—

"She's in Brighton, 'avin' a nice day out. Be 'ome by teatime, she said, so as to dress proper for the concert. Ever such a one for royalty, she is, and no end pleased at the chance to see 'Is 'Ighness."

It was time to turn this all over to the police. I picked up the phone.

"Inspector Morrison? I'm so sorry, Mrs. Martin, he's following up a lead in Sheffield. Shall I try to reach him, or would you like to talk to someone else? We're a bit shorthanded, what with the visit and all, but I could try—"

"No, it's all right. Nothing that can't wait." At any rate, it would have to. Now there was nothing for it but to wait for Mrs. Finch.

THE FIRST ONE in the cathedral when it opened for the concert, I waited by the door in an agony of apprehension until a hat appeared that even I found amazing.

"Mrs. Finch! Ada, I mean, sorry. I'm so glad I saw you. You look splendid."

She preened herself. The bright blue silk dress was a trifle tight, and the hat had probably been worn to weddings since the fifties.

"Ta, dearie." Her hand brushed one of the ostrich feathers and set it trembling, shedding a trifle in the process. "Wot I say is, 'ee may not've been quite the gent to 'is wife, but 'ee 'ad a lot to put up with, dint 'ee? An' still an' all, 'ee's the next king, an' we owes 'im respect."

I stayed by her side as we walked up the aisle, not trying to deal with her views on royal infidelity. "Do you have anyone to sit with? Would you mind if I keep you company?"

She looked gratified at that, but doubtful. "I'd like that, I'm sure, dearie, but the seats is reserved, you know. Mine is—" she looked at her ticket again "—is down this row 'ere. Where's yours?"

"Oh, it's up front somewhere. I'll bet whoever is sitting next to you wouldn't mind trading with me." And if they did, I wasn't above a bribe. Of course, if there were two people together, on both sides of her, we'd have trouble. But I'd manage it somehow. I intended to stick to Ada Finch like glue, if I had to sit on the floor.

I didn't have to. The scholarly looking man who had the seat to Ada's left was delighted to move up twenty or so rows. We settled ourselves, and I encouraged Ada to tell me about her day in Brighton. More important matters would have to wait until later, preferably with Alan present.

And then it was "God Save the Queen," not the shortened version that sometimes precedes or follows a performance, but a full rendition in Charles's honor, and Ada, full of bliss, finally saw him. I felt better, too—I'd spotted Alan just behind him in the VIP section.

I imagine the concert was superb. The orchestra, the choir, the soprano, the violinist all were of the very first rank. I didn't hear a note. The wallet was burning a hole in my pocketbook. What was Alan going to say? How were we going to prove the case against Benson now that I'd messed up the chain of evidence? Did Ada really have the missing stone from his ring, and had he figured that out yet? If this blasted concert would just end so I could get to Alan! I looked at my watch for the tenth time: seven forty-five.

They were playing the last selection, a Mozart thing I should have enjoyed, when I saw him. He was sitting on the other side of the aisle, two rows ahead, and he wasn't paying attention to the music either. His eyes scanned the crowd, and as I watched, he glanced over his shoulder and spotted Ada's hat.

Benson. Back in town and loaded for bear.

I looked away as fast as I could, but not before he'd seen me see him.

His look was three parts malice and one part sheer satisfaction. Oh, dear God. He knew I had his wallet. He'd talked to Mrs. Hawkins.

And he knew Ada had the rest of the evidence that would help convict him of two murders.

I looked around frantically for help, but there was no help. Only the crowd, the blessed, slow-to-move crowd that surrounded us. And the social conventions that decree one does not make a scene in the middle of a concert.

Especially not when royalty is present. There was that. All those unobtrusive policemen around—we stood a very good chance, after all!

"I will follow upon mine enemies and overtake them . . ." Or, in this case, I would escape mine enemy, and Ada with me, until I could get the proper authorities to overtake him. We'd get out of there the very moment the music ended, and we'd sit locked up in my house until Alan came knocking at the door.

Would they never stop playing?

They did, of course, and there was a standing ovation, joined in enthusiastically by Ada, who hadn't followed a note, either, but would go along with anything her prince enjoyed. Then the VIPs were ushered out and we were free to leave.

But all the south doors into the Close were open, and everyone was heading that way, for the reception. I'd forgotten the reception. Damn the reception! We'd edge out along the side of the crowd, my eyes open all the time for Benson, and just go through the Close to my house.

I hadn't counted on the obsession of Ada Finch.

She grasped me by the hand. " 'Urry along, luv! No seats out there. We can get up as close to 'im as we like. Come on, shake a leg there, dearie!" I was towed behind as she elbowed her way through the throng. They were pressing so close, I couldn't see anyone except the people whose feet I was stepping on as we passed.

When she finally panted to a satisfied stop, we were just in front of the dais that had been set up on the grass. On the dais sat Charles, the dean, the bishop, the Lord Mayor, and Alan. Behind us was a mass of humanity that made escape impossible.

And just on the edge of the crowd, at the front and to our right, stood Herbert Benson, pointing toward us and speaking urgently to the constable standing guard.

"Ada, I'm not feeling very well," I stage-whispered. It was true enough. "Let's go home. This way." I tugged to the left.

She remained firmly planted. "Not me, dearie. You go ahead if you've a mind. I'm staying right 'ere."

"No, you have to come, too. It's—please, Ada! Come *now*!"
She just stared at me.

"Oh, all right! It's Benson. I think he thinks you have something he lost in the Town Hall, and I don't think he's going to be very nice about it. Do come before he—"

I finally got through. "The Town 'All?" she said slowly. "Would this be it?"

She opened her handbag and pulled out something very small, laying it in the palm of her other hand. It was black and shiny, like a tiny pool of black water.

It was the onyx from Benson's ring.

I've never fully believed in thought transference, but that night I think Ada read my mind, or part of it.

"Oh, my Gawd!" she said, her voice beginning to rise. " 'Ee musta lost it that night—and that means 'ee—"

She looked at him and screamed.

21

IT WAS ALMOST three in the morning.

"I must go home," said Alan, yawning.

"You'll have to see yourself to the door. I can't move." I was in the biggest chair in my parlor, looking and feeling like a rag doll, dropped there by a careless child. Sam, on the window seat, and Emmy, on the hearth rug, had long since settled themselves for the night.

"Nor can I." He yawned again from the couch and propped one long leg over the other.

"Will they ever let you supervise a royal visit again, do you think? I mean, to say that all hell broke loose is an understatement." Mrs. Finch's scream had brought Benson and the police guards to our side simultaneously, and Benson's furious shouts during the struggle were enough to convict him of a number of things. Prince Charles, of course, had been unceremoniously removed from the scene the moment the fracas began.

He grinned, a little wryly. "At least we caught the villain, and we've got the evidence, and no harm came to the Prince, even if he did have to be hustled out of there rather more quickly than we'd planned."

"We'd have gotten the villain a long time ago if Mrs. Finch hadn't held out on us."

"Morrison did point that out to her." The grin was pure pleasure this time. "She said she was just doing her job and what harm did it do to pick up something pretty for her locket as her son gave her for her birthday, and were we accusing an honest woman of stealing—words to that effect, and lots more. Morrison was totally vanquished."

"All the same, if she'd given it to the police, Barbara Dean might not have died."

"There's never any point in 'if only,' love. And you're not to apologize again for stealing evidence. I'm happy we have him now. He has a lot to answer for."

I accepted Alan's dictum and changed the subject. "I wonder what'll become of the Town Hall."

He shrugged and yawned, his jaws cracking, and struggled out of the couch. The cats twitched their ears and opened sleepy eyes.

"Who knows? Something useful, I hope."

"I know! How about moving the Sherebury Museum there? It would be a perfect place—"

Alan yawned again. "Your next project. I'm for home. Come here."

He held out both his hands, and I managed, after all, to get out of the embrace of the chair and into Alan's.

When he could speak again, he said, "By the way, to answer your question, no, I'll never supervise a royal visit again."

"Alan! Do you mean you're retiring?"

"Not quite yet. I'm being posted away for a few months, starting in September."

"Away where?" I moved out of his arms, disturbed.

"I'm to take over temporarily as commandant of the Police Staff College at Bramshill. Have you heard of it?"

"Heavens, yes! That's where they send the senior officers for special courses. But Alan that's a really important job! Congratulations! Only—"

I stopped.

"Only what?"

"Nothing. I'm really happy for you. That's a wonderful promotion." Emmy and Sam caught my tone of voice and woke fully.

"Only what?" He pulled me back into his embrace.

"I'll—miss you."

"Why?"

"Because I like having you around! Because I—"

"No, I'm not trying to make you say it!" He chuckled. "What I meant was, why need you miss me? Why not come along? It's a Jacobean house, you know, same period as this one but rather larger—about fifty bedrooms, originally. And there's an extremely nice apartment for the commandant and his wife."

"His—wife?" There was something wrong with my breathing.

"Well, we're going to have to do something, aren't we? Because if we see much more of each other, one evening neither of us is going to want me to leave, and it would never do for a chief constable and a respectable American lady . . ."

"No, it wouldn't, would it?"

There was an interval.

"Alan, I—"

"It's all right. Don't answer me now. I really am going home, because my driver's waiting and I daren't shock him." He gave me one more very proficient kiss and Emmy, jealous, twined herself around his ankles. "I'll ring you in the morning—well, afternoon, perhaps, when you've had a chance for some sleep. We never had that carouse, did we?"

"No, Mrs. Finch and Benson between them canceled those

plans. And I'd enjoy a really wild evening with you. But, Alan, what I was about to say is, I—I'm not sure I'm ready for marriage quite yet. But—well, even the cats seem to approve of the general idea."

Half an hour later, as his car drove decorously up a sleeping Monkswell Street, the first hint of dawn's gray appeared in the eastern sky, and somewhere, tentatively, a lark began to sing.

TOWN HALL

THE HIG

THE
FEATHERS

SHERE
CATHE

WOOD'S

TO BRIGHTON

SHEREBURY